CLUES IN THE CLAY

PEARL SANDS BEACH RESORT COZY MYSTERY
BOOK TWO

DANIELLE COLLINS

MILLIE BRIGGS

Fairfield Publishing

CONTENTS

CHARLENE DAVIS, better known as Charlie, glided across the elegant marble tile of the Pearl Sands Resort lobby. The highly polished floor reflected the crystal-and-gold chandelier at its center, adding a touch of gold to the cream-colored backdrop.

While Charlie was still a relatively new employee at the resort, she found herself waving hello and good morning to familiar employees wherever she went. As the hotel's concierge, she focused on growing her community of friends at the resort—not only for her own benefit, seeing as she was a resident of the tied island where Pearl Sands was located, but also to further her job and the cohesion it required from all parts of the resort.

Whether it was a request for an impossible slot at the spa or a reservation at one of the two upscale restaurants the resort boasted, Charlie knew someone who could make those requests happen. She'd fostered those friendships with small gifts, words of encouragement, and offering any favor she could in return, and it was working.

"Morning, Charlie," one of the bellhops said with a wink.

"Morning, Parker," Charlie replied with a smile. The young man carried two large suitcases, one in each hand, muscles bulging beneath his Pearl Sands shirt. "Been busy already, I see?"

"That party taking up a third of the villas is leaving today." He didn't add *thank goodness*, but she heard it in his tone.

"I bet they've kept you guys hopping."

His grin widened. "You could say that."

"Parker, over here!"

He shrugged and lowered his voice. "And they all learned my name the first day."

She knew what that meant. When you were known, you could be called for any—and every—little thing. They'd kept Parker busy, and she only hoped they'd leave him a good tip.

"Hop to it," she laughed.

He groaned but plastered on a smile as he turned around for another load of expensive luggage.

Charlie paused at her desk, jogging her mouse to wake up the screen. She'd just come back from a quick break since she'd started earlier than usual that morning, and now she wanted to check one last thing before her next meeting.

"That's what I thought," she muttered.

"Talking to yourself?"

Charlie jerked back, heart leaping into her throat. "You've got to stop sneaking up on me like that, Nelson."

"Who says I was sneaking?" the man replied with a mischievous gaze.

Charlie took in Nelson Hall, also a resident of Barnabe Island, who lived on the southern half where most of the working-class homes were located. He wore a shirt in muted tans and greens, with palm frond images, over khaki shorts with boat shoes. The gray at his temples only made the rest of his brown hair look darker, and she caught the hint of a day's growth of hair against his chin, the rebellious stubble defying the days he had spent in the military.

"Maybe I'm just so focused on planning for our meeting I didn't think to look for you here in the villa?" She grinned so he would know she was kidding and then went back to the information she was looking up.

"I know, I'm early, but I was bored at the shop." Charlie pictured the inside of *Ceramica*—an upscale pottery boutique located in the Luxury Square shops minutes from the resort—and could imagine how easily Nelson could get bored there. While he could afford to have a shop in the expensive retail area, he fit best with the working-class residents of the tied island.

"You realize you're being ridiculous, right? You're the one who chose to open the place." Charlie grinned up at him and caught his responding smile.

"I know. I mean, I could just close the shop instead of being bored there…"

He was goading her, she knew it, but she had other things on her mind. "Come on. We've got a date with some coffee and business to discuss."

"Did you say date?"

Despite her calm composure, Charlie knew her cheeks reflected the heat of embarrassment. She spun on her heel. "Come on, you."

They wove through the mass of guests checking out as well as other staff going about their morning duties. She led him down a back hallway reserved for staff, assuming her boss wouldn't mind Nelson's presence, and led them out past the three pools of the inner courtyard to a small café at the back of the resort.

The Seaside Café got its name from location, but it held up to scrutiny with drinks named for all things nautical and seaworthy. Charlie ordered a Portside Latte, which was basically a latte with vanilla, and Nelson requested the Anemone Espresso, which was espresso with cinnamon.

Charlie enjoyed the slight breeze coming in off the ocean through the open glass doors that slid into pockets in the walls. It created a type of 'outdoor inside' feeling that added to the charm of the walkup café adjacent to the beach.

Nelson examined the various cups for sale until the barista called out their drinks and then they moved to a small table that looked out toward the ocean.

"Thanks for the drink," he said, toasting her with his small double-walled espresso cup.

"Thank the resort," she said with a smile. "This is business, of course." Charlie cringed at her need to remind him of that, but his earlier comment had stuck with her.

Nelson was one of the first people who had befriended her during her initial week at the Pearl Sands and, while he was handsome and kind, he was also a flirt. While harmless, she wasn't sure he meant his comments as anything more than playful jabs, but she'd decided early on to treat them as such.

Still, when she looked up and caught his hazel-eyed gaze in the sunlight, she remembered his support that first week. He'd offered wisdom during a difficult case she hadn't expected to work, seeing as she'd come to the Pearl Sands to be a concierge and not a private investigator, like she'd been most of her life.

"What?" Nelson said.

She realized she'd been staring. Time to get back to business. "I wanted to run over the details of your class and go over the supplies list one more time. I think I have everything taken care of, but I'd like to be positive before tomorrow."

He laughed, the sound warm and rich. "You're more detailed than my drill sergeant."

"I'll take that as a compliment."

He took another sip of his espresso. "I'm planning on having space for twelve people—that's still a good number?"

"Yes." Charlie checked her worksheet. "I have ten signed up, but we have a new wave of guests coming in today that I was going to pitch the class to. I'm positive we can fill those last two slots before tomorrow."

"There's no need to fill them," he reminded her.

"I know. I just promised you twelve and—"

Nelson's hand rested on hers. "Charlie, is everything okay?"

She jerked her hand back and met his gaze. "What do you mean?"

"You're...tense."

"I'm not."

"You kind of are."

She took a deep breath. She had been on edge that morning since she'd realized her three-month review was coming up and, as ridiculous as it sounded, she felt pressure to prove to her boss that she'd done what he asked of the concierge program—and more.

"It's that review, isn't it?" Nelson guessed.

She'd forgotten that she'd mentioned her nerves about it the last time she'd had her friends over for dinner the week prior.

"I suppose it's weighing on me a little." The admission felt good and reminded her that Nelson was, above all, her friend.

"You're going to nail it. You know Felipe, he all but worships the ground you walk on."

Charlie laughed and shook her head, despite the fact that Nelson's description of her boss wasn't far off. "I think it's just that I met him before being an employee, you know? This review feels almost *more* important because I want to prove to him he made the right choice in hiring me."

"You will." Nelson nodded once, as if deciding it would be so, and then shifted his focus back to the sheets of paper she'd brought. "Let's talk about clay."

She let him change the subject for her benefit, and her muscles relaxed as she focused on the numbers and the space she'd need the event staff to set up for Nelson's pottery class. It was one of her first big initiatives at the Pearl Sands, offering an interactive class with a local artisan, and she was determined to make sure it was successful.

She was going to make sure this class went off without a hitch no matter what.

———

CHARLIE CHECKED HER WATCH. It was almost time for her next meeting, though she wasn't sure if the couple had checked in yet. She'd gotten an email from Will Chrisman asking to set up a time to talk with her upon their arrival. From what she could gather, they were coming to the Pearl Sands for a week-long honeymoon, and he wanted to make it as special as possible for his new bride.

She picked up the ivory-and-gold handle of her desk phone and pressed a button for the front desk.

"Hello, Miss Charlie, how can I help you?" a deep voice boomed across the line.

"Hey, Elijah." Charlie felt the smile tug at her lips.

She loved when she got connected to Elijah and how he called her *miss* even if she was well past the age where that was appropriate. Then again, he was one of the oldest workers at the Pearl Sands and had worked there since he was a teen. Elijah had started as a bellhop and done nearly every job imaginable before landing at the front desk, where he said he'd stay until he died—if Felipe would allow it. "Did the Chrismans call about a late check-in?"

"Let me check," he said. She looked up to see him confer with the others at the check-in desk. While she had access to check-in information, sometimes notes from calls weren't entered into the electronic system.

She could have walked over to talk to him, but she didn't want to be away from her desk if her appointment showed up.

"Looks like our system is slow. They checked in, and Parker showed them to their suite. Did you want me to call them?"

"That's odd that it's not registering here. Thank you, Elijah. I'll wait for them here. I've got no one scheduled after them anyway."

"You got it, Miss Charlie. Anything else I can do for you?"

"Nope, you've been a gem—as always."

"Bye now."

She hung up in time to see a couple emerge from the hallway to the elevators, and something about the way they looked at each other clued her in to the fact that this was likely her afternoon appointment. They looked like a couple in love.

"Mr. and Mrs. Chrisman?"

The woman giggled and hid her face against her husband's shoulder, a blanket of blonde hair covering her soft features. "I just love the sound of that."

The man, a little older than his young wife, smiled down at her before meeting Charlie's gaze. "Hi, yes, we're the

Chrismans." His own goofy smile indicated he felt the same way as his wife. "We've got an appointment."

"Have a seat and welcome to the Pearl Sands," Charlie said, indicating the two luxury wingback chairs that faced her across the desk.

"Thanks," he said, holding out the seat for his wife before taking his own. "We'd like to get some excursions scheduled for this week."

"But not too many," the woman said. Her blush deepened as she looked back at her new husband.

Charlie went over her notes. It was Will and...Monica. She made a mental note of the woman's name. "You've got it. Just a few things to break up your stay here?" Charlie asked.

"Yeah, that sounds good," Will said.

"Is there anything romantic going on?" Monica asked.

Charlie pondered the question then smiled as things fell into place. "What about a pottery class?"

"Perfect!" Monica said.

"No way," Will said at the same time as his wife.

They looked at each other and laughed.

"Will, you know I love *Ghost*. It's one of my favorite movies. Please can we do the class?"

"I can assure you this class will be perfect for all skill levels. The presenter is a very successful local artisan with a shop in Luxury Square, and this is his first class here. It's sure to be a highlight." Charlie held herself back from pushing the class any further but grinned as she saw the man's resolve falter.

"Fine," Will finally said. "Anything for you, my wife."

Monica giggled and accepted his quick kiss before turning back to Charlie. "We're in."

"Wonderful. And how about a sunset ocean cruise with dinner and—" She looked back at her screen. "—a couples massage?"

"Now those things I can get behind," Will said.

Charlie looked to the wife. "I'm good with that too," Monica said with a nod.

Charlie went through the particulars of booking them when a ringtone from Will's pocket interrupted them.

"Sorry, I've got to take this. Be right back, babe." Will stalked off, phone moving to his ear as if it belonged there.

"Sorry, he's on the verge of big career news. That could be it right now."

"I hope it's good news," Charlie said with a smile.

"Me too."

"When did you two get married?"

"Two weeks ago," Monica admitted. "I wanted to leave for our honeymoon right away, but Will had stuff to finish up for work, you know? He's supposed to keep his phone in the room, but hopefully this is the call he needed."

"I hope so too," Charlie agreed.

Charlie went through the rest of the details with Monica and then sent the couple on their way with a printed itinerary on high quality stationary with the Pearl Sands resort logo embossed in gold at the top.

"They looked happy," a voice said.

Charlie looked up to see her friend—Valentina Lopez, the head of housekeeping—slide into the seat Monica had just vacated.

"They are, but I'm happy too."

"Oh?"

"I just booked the last two slots in Nelson's pottery class. It's filled and ready to go. What a relief."

"You weren't worried, were you?"

"Of course I was," Charlie said with a sigh.

"You know Felipe isn't going to judge you based on one class's attendance." Valentina gave her a compassionate look.

"You've been talking to Nelson."

Valentina laughed. "He may have mentioned you seemed stressed. Here's a cupcake."

Charlie grinned and accepted the carrot cake cupcake Otto, the resort's pastry chef, had made. The cream cheese frosting was the perfect amount of tangy sweetness juxtaposed to the spongey cake. She took a bite and sighed in contentment. "Perfection."

"Happy to oblige. Hey, that couple wasn't the Chrismans, was it?"

Charlie licked her lips and wiped at the corners of her mouth with the napkin Valentina had brought. "Yes. Why do you ask?"

"Do you know who Will is?"

Charlie frowned. "No, but I know he's on a honeymoon with his wife."

"I wouldn't have known either, but my brother, Michael, manages a local art gallery."

"I didn't know that. How does this connect?" Charlie asked.

"Michael told me that a well-known artist was going to be here at the resort this week—based on a magazine article, I guess. Naturally, I had to look up who it is."

"Will?"

"Yes." She lowered her voice, leaning forward so as not to spread the information through the lobby. "Rumor has it he's going to shift focus from physical art to digital. He's just waiting on a big deal to go through with an online gallery."

"Okay." Charlie wasn't sure how she felt about digital art.

"You're not impressed." Valentina crossed her arms and offered a raised eyebrow. "My brother says that it's the upset of the Florida art world right now."

A laugh behind them startled both women, and Charlie looked up into the face of a guest she didn't recognize. He was tall with black hair and a strong jaw that looked tense.

"I'd hardly say that," a deep voice said.

"I'm sorry, sir, did you need the concierge?" Valentina asked.

Charlie caught the faint blush on her friends' cheeks at being overheard gushing about a guest as she quickly vacated her seat.

"Oh, no, thanks though. I was just going to ask where the nearest restaurant is?"

Charlie plastered on the smile she'd grown accustomed to using with guests and pointed out the direction to the man. She watched as he reached for the hand of a beautiful woman in a tight dress and high heels. She was looking at her reflection in her phone before taking a photo with the man, pressing her face up close to his.

Valentina slipped back into the chair and shook her head. "How embarrassing."

"You were just expressing something your brother said." She checked around them. "He was the one listening in."

"True, but still."

Charlie knew what she meant. It was one thing to share gossip with a friend in the staff lounge and another to be caught while on the resort floor.

"I'd better get going. We've got a meeting in five, but I wanted you to enjoy that cupcake fresh."

"You're the best," Charlie said, taking another delicate bite and trying not to get frosting on her nose.

Valentina waved and took off toward the staff hall. Charlie watched her go, thinking about what the man had said. He hadn't appeared to be eavesdropping on purpose, but it seemed as if he knew something about Will and his career.

Charlie made a mental note to keep herself apprised of the situation, and to talk to some of the housekeeping staff who seemed to have ears everywhere. If there was the potential that the honeymoon couple could face a guest who was antagonistic toward them, she wanted to ensure that didn't happen.

It was, after all, her job to make sure everyone had a wonderful stay at the Pearl Sands.

2

───────

"THE WEATHER COULDN'T BE BETTER, DON'T you think?" Nelson grinned as he looked up to the robin's egg blue sky.

Charlie had to agree. They'd scheduled the pottery class to take part outside in the private pool area, since they could bar entry to those without reservations and there was enough shaded spots to set up the wheels and other equipment Nelson had rented for the class.

"Are you sure being outside will be the best option?" Charlie had tried her best to convince Nelson to host the class inside in one of their conference rooms, but he'd insisted that it needed to be outside.

"Still sure. I mean, you agree the weather is amazing."

She nodded.

"And the scenery is conducive to creativity—or so I think." He checked with her as she offered a begrudging shrug. "Then I see no reason to go inside where it'll be cold and impersonal. Maybe if the weather gets bad for our next class, but best to be outside whenever possible."

She laughed. "I think that may be your motto."

He shrugged and winked at her. "I think you're right."

They moved through the gated area and Charlie made sure to shut the barrier behind her, a sign noting the closure of the pool for a private event. The pool's beautiful blue water remained smooth and untouched, and she saw the rows of chairs and wheels set up.

"Do you have everything you need?" Charlie knew that Nelson had come early that morning to unload with the help of one of the groundskeepers, but she wanted to check every last detail.

"We are set to go. You have the refreshments handled, right?"

"Yes, the staff will be setting them up in—" She checked her watch. "—probably ten minutes."

"Perfect. I think that should be it."

They stood there, the sun warming their shoulders, as Nelson looked over everything with a trained eye. Charlie waited to see if he thought of anything else.

She counted the seats out of habit, but started a bit at the number she reached. Counting them again she turned to him. "Why are there thirteen seats?"

"One's for you." He turned to look at her, his expression open. "I mean, it's our first class and I figured you should take it too."

"Why?"

"Because you need to know what you're selling."

She frowned. "It's not like I need to know how to throw pottery to be able to recommend the experience to someone."

"Perhaps, but I think it will make you more effective if you do."

"I didn't take the time off to do this."

"Already cleared it with Felipe."

Charlie's eyebrows rose. "You did?"

"I did."

She narrowed her gaze at him, trying to gauge if he was lying or not. Seeing no signs of deception, she let out a soft sigh. "I don't think it's...me."

"What's that supposed to mean?" he laughed.

"The clay." She wrinkled her nose. "Not something I want to get my hands in."

"The great P.I. Charlene Davis doesn't want to get her hands dirty with *clean* clay?"

"I'm no longer a P.I., you know that, and I'm not great at anything. Besides, I have certain..." She fumbled for the word. "Standards."

"Come on, Charlie." Nelson nudged her with his shoulder. "What if you don't have to touch the clay, you just take the class to observe?"

She considered this. She really didn't think she'd like the feeling of the clay and also knew she wasn't creative in the way it would take to come up with a pottery piece. Still, sitting through the class as a type of audit to know how to better offer it to the resort guests did sound like a smart idea.

"If you promise I don't have to touch the clay...."

"You don't," he said, crossing his heart with a grin.

"Then I'll join."

"Good." His smile brightened. "There'll be plenty of time to convince you to try real pottery, but for now, at least you'll know how the class runs."

She nodded just as the staff access door to the kitchen opened and some of the kitchen staff began rolling out carts of refreshments. They'd decided to include beverages and snacks for this first class, though they had already tossed around the idea of offering one of the classes at night along with dinner. It would be a perfect date night for resort guests.

"We're almost ready," she said, rubbing her hands together. "I'll go open up the gate and welcome the attendees as they enter."

"Perfect. I plan on starting a few minutes late unless all are here."

She nodded as they parted ways and made her way back to the gate where she welcomed the Fitzgeralds, an older couple spending two weeks at the Pearl Sands who had been overjoyed to hear about the new class option.

"I can't tell you how excited I am," Mrs. Fitzgerald said. She was beaming, and her husband chuckled behind her.

"She really is," he said. "We've been coming to the Peal Sands for years now, and they've never offered anything like this."

"I'm so glad to hear you're both looking forward to the class. Mr. Hall is inside, he's the owner of *Ceramica* and will be hosting the class. Please feel free to go in and say hello."

"Oh, that's perfect. Come on, honey, let's go."

Mr. Fitzgerald winked at Charlie, and they moved past just as another guest arrived. He was younger than the couple and had the look of a businessman about him, but he'd been the one to come up to Charlie to reserve a spot at the class without her having to offer it first. The rest of the attendees trickled in until the only ones missing were the honeymooners.

Charlie checked her watch. It was almost ten minutes past their intended start time, and she was about to go tell Nelson to start without them, when she caught sight of the couple making their way across the pool deck toward her. They held hands and were more concerned about one another, pausing every few steps to steal a kiss.

"Hello," she said, trying her best not to let her impatience show as they came closer to the gate.

"This the class?" Will said.

"We're so ready," Monica said with a giggle. Charlie caught sight of the glass of orange liquid in the woman's hand and the faint whiff of alcohol on her breath. Apparently, she had enjoyed one too many cocktails with breakfast.

"Welcome. Come on in and we'll find you your seats. The potter is about to begin."

"I'm so excited," Monica said as she squeezed past Charlie into the pool area with Will trailing behind.

Charlie walked behind him, flinching when it looked like Monica might tip over into the pool. She reached out, but Will caught his wife by the arm and gently pulled her back to him.

"Welcome," Nelson said, standing up from where he'd begun his introduction to the group. "Your seats are at the back."

"Nice," Will said with a huffed laugh. "I'm always at the back."

"Shhh. I'm excited for this, Will," Monica said, her whisper coming out much louder than Charlie thought she meant it to.

Charlie took her seat behind the honeymooners and tried her best to follow along with Nelson's introduction to pottery. From a show of hands, most of those in the class had worked with pottery before and were willing to get their hands dirty as soon as possible. Only Will and Monica failed to reply to Nelson's questions. Charlie had to assume they didn't have experience and had a feeling Nelson would spend most of his time with them.

As he walked down the aisle to deliver clay to the eager hands of the class members, Charlie found herself distracted by Will and Monica. She was giggling uncontrollably and trying to remain quiet, but it wasn't helping that Will continued to steal kisses.

Nelson stopped in front of them, and Charlie watched from her seat behind. She wondered how he would handle the distracting couple, but she shouldn't have worried. He explained that they could start on the clay now even though they had no experience, and Monica was more than willing to jump in.

Charlie watched as Nelson helped her throw the clay onto the wheel and showed her what to do. Her focus seemed to sharpen with the action of the spinning wheel, and she shoved off Will's advances to recreate the scene from Ghost with an actual whispered admonishment. She was into the pottery, and Charlie could tell it made a difference to her attention.

"You sure I can't convince you to try some clay on the wheel? I rented that just for you."

"I'm sure." Charlie laughed, looking up at Nelson, who continually surprised her. He ran two shops on the island —one boasting extremely expensive pieces for the upscale clients that Luxury Square attracted, and one with smaller items, some more practical, in his shop on the south side of the island. Anyone could purchase those pieces, and Charlie knew she would grab something from that shop once she could replenish her savings from the furniture she'd bought when she first moved into her cottage here.

"Well, maybe next time."

She didn't want to break it to him that the next time she wouldn't be attending the class at all, but before she could say anything, Monica stood up and threw a handful of clay at Will.

"You never let me do anything fun. You ruin it all! You're just like him!" Bursting into tears, she wiped her clay-coated fingers on the provided apron before ripping it off and storming out of the pool area.

Charlie felt her mouth go dry as every eye turned toward Will.

"I— Sorry, folks. I'll go make sure she's okay." Will stood and rushed off, leaving Charlie at the receiving end of the rest of the glances.

Nelson saved her from having to reply by calling their attention to the front, but she had lost her ability to focus on anything he was saying.

Part of Charlie felt bad for the young woman, who'd clearly had too much to drink that morning and was facing a difficult task like pottery without a clear head. On the other hand, her words bothered Charlie. What had she meant by telling her new husband that he was "just like him." Who was *him*?

Charlie knew she wouldn't be able to focus and stood quietly, slipping away from the class without a backward glance. She needed to see if the couple was planning on coming back to the class, but more than anything, Charlie wanted to make sure that Monica was all right.

THE SUN REFLECTED off the main pool, making Charlie squint. She covered her eyes with her hand and scanned the area for Monica. The woman couldn't have gone too far, though it was possible she had headed straight back to her villa.

She moved toward the middle area, stepping around guests lounging in reclining chairs and young twenty-somethings splashing in the pool. The scent of sunscreen mingled with chlorine and created a distinctively summer scent that felt at home in Florida, while the rest of the country emerged into spring.

Looking closer toward the bar area that separated the two main pools in the resort's center courtyard, Charlie caught sight of a tall, blond man—Will. He wasn't who she was looking for, but she reasoned that he'd found his wife, though she couldn't see who he was speaking with.

Three young women clad in bikinis passed her, laughing and talking, and when she stepped into the covered outdoor hallway, she caught sight of who Will was talking to. It was not Monica.

Her eyes narrowed as she recognized the other man. He'd been the one to disparage Will's art the previous day. She'd wondered at the time if he'd known Will, and the way in which they were speaking seemed to confirm that. Both men wore intense expressions, though Will seemed to show an underlying thread of anger beneath their controlled conversation.

The other man was tall and, by a younger woman's standards, handsome. He had a model-like quality to the way he stood—at once casual and practiced. His white shirt was unbuttoned further than was normally acceptable and showed off chiseled abs and a flawless tan. Will, in contrast, looked red from the sun and stood several inches shorter than the man.

Charlie considered getting closer, but it seemed as if the tone had shifted away from outright anger to intense discussion. She wondered if perhaps she'd misjudged their initial dislike for passionate subject matter, but she wasn't sure that was the case.

25

She took a few steps closer, keeping her distance by staying in the hallway with a few barriers and planters of palms between them. Her next step opened up a wider line of sight, and that was when she saw her.

Monica was on the opposite side of the pool area on a lounge chair with another drink in hand, crying her eyes out. Charlie's heart constricted at the sight, and she quickly forgot the men and whatever problems they were hashing out.

While Charlie knew she was the furthest thing from an expert on relationship woes, she had dealt with a myriad of people struggling with domestic disputes. This wasn't serious, not like the ones she'd handled as a New York cop, but perhaps she could be a listening ear for the woman.

Charlie stopped at the bar and requested a coffee with cream and sugar from the young man working there and then made her way toward the woman. Her dark hair spilled over her shoulders in beachy waves, and her whole body shook with silent tears. Monica shoved her expensive sunglasses up on her forehead and, after discarding her drink on a nearby table, she dropped her face into her hands.

"Monica?" Charlie spoke low and quietly, hoping not to startle the young woman.

She looked up for a moment, eyes teary and red, before burying her face again. "I'm not having a great morning."

It wasn't a brushoff, but it also wasn't an invitation, so Charlie pressed. "May I sit?"

Monica didn't answer, but Charlie watched as her shoulders rose and fell. She'd take that as a yes.

Charlie observed what she could about the young woman. She was beautiful, stunning really, with long, lean limbs, curves in the right places, and a natural beauty that wasn't reliant on makeup. In fact, that was one thing Charlie had noticed about the woman when they'd come to her desk. She'd worn no makeup and her skin was flawless.

"Is there anything I can do to help you?"

Monica took in a deep breath and wiped at her eyes. She wore a one-piece swimsuit with shorts over it and, as she leaned back, Charlie caught the red lines against white where her strap had shifted. It looked like she and her husband had spent time in the sun the day before.

"Thanks, but I'll be okay." She drew in a deep breath and let it out.

"I'm guessing this is about more than just your clay bowl."

The mention of the incident brought more tears, but Monica wiped them away. "Yeah. I mean, I've known Will for several years now and he's a good man, but sometimes, I just feel like he's so selfish. This is our honeymoon and I just wanted to do pottery, you know?"

She reached for the glass that Charlie assumed was a mimosa, but Charlie held out the coffee. "How about some of this?"

The woman blushed. "I guess I should cut back on the alcohol so early in the day, huh?"

"I think you'd feel better at the moment with some caffeine," Charlie said.

Monica sipped the coffee and seemed to relax. "I'm a graphic designer— Well, I'm going to be."

Charlie tried to follow the woman's logic, but rather than say anything, let her speak.

"I was a model before," Monica continued. "When I married Will, I knew that life was over. I wanted it to be, you know? And my degree was in design so I figured, let's do that. The pottery class was just, like, this perfect opportunity to try my hand at art. Not digital, but something real. And look how that turned out."

"It's our first class." Charlie slipped into her own somber mood. "It was my idea, actually. My friend is the potter— Nelson—and I thought, 'How fun would this be to offer the resort guests' but maybe I was wrong about that." She gave a self-deprecating laugh.

"No," Monica reached across and gripped Charlie's hand. "It *was* a good idea. I think everyone there is having a great time. It was just me, drinking too much, and Will— only focused on me—that messed it up for you. Gosh, I'm sorry about that."

Charlie felt the woman's sincerity and smiled. "That's kind of you. Maybe I can ask Nelson to give you a private lesson. If you really want to learn about pottery, I'm pretty certain he wouldn't mind. He's very passionate about what he does."

"I checked out his shop in the Luxury Square. It's impressive. I think I'd like to try again, if he doesn't mind."

Charlie smiled back at her. "I'll see what I can do. I think we'll be leaving the pottery equipment up anyway so it shouldn't be too hard to fit in a private session."

"Thanks..." She looked at Charlie's name badge. "Charlie." Her grin showed some of the aftereffects of the alcohol she'd had that morning, but there was a clarity there too.

"Will you and your new husband be okay?"

The question seemed to surprise Monica, but she didn't appear to mind. "I think so." Her gaze roamed the pool area and Charlie joined her in the search, though she had an advantage knowing where he'd been before.

She scanned that area, but he and the other man were gone. It was only then that Charlie caught sight of another man. He was tall, older than both Will and Monica, and appeared distinguished in a dark blazer and slacks. He stood almost exactly opposite them, and his focus was solely on Monica.

Charlie was about to ask the woman if she knew him, but he slipped behind a pillar and disappeared.

"Thanks for talking with me, Charlie, but I think I'm going back to our villa for a nap."

"Are you sure everything is all right?" Charlie pressed.

"Yeah. I mean, Will is under a lot of pressure right now and, while this is our honeymoon, I knew he would have to conduct some business while we were here. I think maybe I convinced myself he'd do that the first day and give me the rest of the week, but…I guess I was wrong."

Charlie felt for the woman who had to share her honeymoon with her husband's business, but it was clear she had also agreed to it.

"I hope today gets better for you," Charlie said, standing. "If there is anything I can do, just call the concierge desk. I'll also get your private lesson on the books and send you an email when it's scheduled."

"Thank you," Monica said with a smile. Then, coffee in hand, she headed toward the private villas at the south end of the resort.

Charlie watched her go. No one followed her, and Will was nowhere in sight. She hoped the young woman could rest and regain some of her day. It was a shame to be miserable in paradise.

3

La Cantina was filled to the brim with patrons and loud music. Colorful piñatas, decorative sombreros, and all manner of Mexican art cluttered the walls, giving the place a lived-in, homey feel. The scent of spicy salsa and fried tortilla chips permeated the air and made Charlie's stomach grumble.

The rest of her day had gone as planned, more or less, and the remainder of the pottery class had also gone off without a hitch. Charlie experienced a mix of pride and trepidation wondering what could happen next to attack the first big project she'd started in her new role.

When Nelson suggested they meet up to talk about it over dinner, Charlie had agreed. Though now, as she wove through the mass of bodies of the tied island's southern residents, she wondered if this was a meeting or a date.

She'd thrown on a comfortable black cotton dress and strappy sandals, but she hadn't taken any extra time for her hair or makeup. There'd been no chance to anyway, since she'd worked late on several large parties that were coming in the next week and had requested outings that required detailed plans.

"Evening," a deep voice said behind her.

She spun to see Nelson. He wore his trademark printed shirt open over a white t-shirt, shorts, and sandals. He was the epitome of casual and relaxed, which was something she admired about him.

"I'm not late, am I?"

"Right on time." Nelson's smile widened, and Charlie forced herself to look away.

He was handsome, there was no way around that, but she'd only been at the Pearl Sands for a short time and wasn't looking to get involved—with anyone.

"Will we be able to find a table?" She laughed as everyone around them exuded life and energy.

"Follow me." Nelson wrapped his hand around hers and pulled her through the crowd.

Charlie felt the heat from his fingers wind their way up her arm, but she focused on the fact that he didn't want to lose her in the crowd. And it was a crowd. There were men in work shirts and pants, women whom Charlie recognized as part of the housekeeping staff at the resort, and other residents of the southern end of Barnabe Island who made their living in the small village there.

It was clear to her after her first month at the Pearl Sands that this end of the tied island was her favorite. There were people here who she could fit in with, which was a stark contrast to the northern side of the island where Luxury Square was located—as well as the homes of the wealthy that lined the rest of the slip until the land bridge that connected it to the mainland.

"Here we are," Nelson said, pulling her through the door to the outside patio covered in bistro lights and just as packed as inside, expect for a small table in the corner that had a reserved sign on it. "Gustavo reserved this for me."

"Aren't you lucky," Charlie said with a laugh as he held the wrought iron chair out for her.

She sunk into the deep cushion and exhaled. It was the perfect night to be outside, and she had to admit the atmosphere of the patio was even better than inside. On the edge of the square area covered by pavers, colorful paper lanterns hung along with decorative coconuts and carved pieces of art on the exterior wall of the restaurant.

"I am lucky." Nelson's gaze burned into hers, and she shifted under it.

"How did the rest of the class go?" She'd gone back after her talk with Monica and was impressed to see the level of progress the class had made in her absence.

"I think all but one person had thrown before, which made my job easy. They were actually an advanced bunch. Made it fun for me. I'll be firing their pieces soon. I've got a list of who's leaving when so I can make sure everything is done. Do you mind if we keep that space set up for a few days?"

"That's fine. We don't have a private party there until next week and..." She met his gaze. "I was hoping you could do a private lesson for the woman who left today?"

"Will her husband be joining us?" Nelson shook his head good-naturedly.

"I don't think so."

"Then yes, I'd be happy to."

Charlie was relieved. She would have to check with Felipe, who liked to leave that pool open for guests with smaller children when possible, but he would understand. Or so she hoped.

"You'll just owe me." Nelson leaned his elbows on the table and winked.

Charlie was about to reply when the waitress showed up.

"What can I get you? Ah, hello, Miss Charlie," Telma said. The Cuban woman had striking features and a warm smile, but Charlie saw the underlying stress.

"Is everything all right?" she asked.

Telma smiled, relaxing some. "We've had some guests from the resort—" She barely contained her disdain. "—that have been difficult. Mateo had to come out and break up a fight. It's been a long night already."

"I'm so sorry to hear that," Charlie said. She felt the urge to step in—to do something—but knew it wasn't her place. While the residents had started to warm up to her, likely due to her friendship with Nelson, she was still an outsider *and* someone who worked at the resort. She had to prove to them that she was an ally.

"It's okay. What can I get you both?"

They ordered and, as the young woman walked away, Charlie turned back to Nelson. "You've got a soft heart for someone who was a New York cop," he said.

"How did you know that?" Charlie thought back through their conversations over the last few months. While they had become friendly, they hadn't had the chance to go very deep in their conversations. Charlie didn't mind it, seeing as she and Valentina had shared more of their life stories with one another, and that had filled the void of friendship Charlie had felt, but it was clear Nelson had dug deeper.

"I have my ways."

Charlie took a sip of the water Telma had brought. "I don't know how I feel about that."

"Feel honored that I wanted to look into you."

She wrinkled her nose. "More like I feel invaded."

"You shouldn't." He looked around the patio and then back to her. "I didn't do much more than ask a few questions. I like to know who's on the island."

She narrowed her gaze. "I told you I was a P.I. before."

"I know, but anyone can say that."

She rolled her eyes. "And solving the case a few months back? That was, what, a fluke?"

He laughed, the sound deep and genuine. "Perhaps."

Bembe, the teen who worked at *La Cantina* most days, raced up to their table with a cup of homemade salsa and a basket of freshly fried chips. "Hola."

"Hello, Bembe," Charlie said, reaching for a chip.

He looked like he wanted to linger and talk, but Telma called out his name and, with a small wave, he rushed back to the kitchen.

"He's a good kid," Nelson said, loading up a chip with salsa.

"Don't distract me, Hall."

He laughed, covering his full mouth until he swallowed. "Don't be mad, Charlie, I only wanted to get a feeling for your background. Call it a hazard of the job."

"You mean your past job in the Army?"

"Touché. I suppose I do owe you a bit of an explanation."

Charlie's eyebrows rose. She'd tried to approach this topic with him before when he'd stayed late after a dinner party she'd hosted for him, Valentina, and her husband Stephen. Nelson had stayed behind to help her clean up. She'd asked about his military career, but he'd been tightlipped. She'd taken the hint.

Was it possible he would open up to her? And if so, why now?

"I was in the Army for a good part of my life. Went in at eighteen and committed fully. I loved the rigidity of it, if you can believe that."

It was hard for her to see him like that as opposed to his relaxed appearance now, but appearances were not always the full truth.

"I had been in for a while when I decided I really wanted to go CID."

"What's that again?" Charlie took another chip, dipping it in the salsa.

"Criminal Investigation Division. It was perfect for me. I have a mind that likes to solve puzzles—as I assume you do—and I thrived under their training. I had some hard cases, but in all, I'd say my career was well suited to me and I excelled."

"Why'd you get out then?"

"You're assuming I did."

"Well..." She gestured at him. "You're a potter with two shops and you live on Barnabe Island."

"Fair point." A pained look came over him. "I decided my time was up when I'd been in for about twenty years. I was nearing forty and I thought maybe I wanted to do something different. At the time, I was thinking about things I'd missed out on—a relationship, time with my parents who were getting older, kids, things like that."

Charlie nodded. She could understand the desire for things that you felt like you'd missed when everyone else had them.

"I was honorably discharged and went to work for a private company." Now she could clearly see the lines on his forehead as if they signaled the storm inside. "I don't talk about that time—not with anyone—but I will say that I thought I was doing the right thing at the time."

Charlie opened her mouth but was interrupted by the delivery of their food by a waitress she didn't know. Nelson thanked the woman in Spanish and then met Charlie's gaze.

"I know you want to ask questions, and maybe someday I'll be willing to tell you more, but I can't—I can't talk about it now."

Charlie saw the pain etched onto his handsome features. She resonated with it so deeply that it frightened her. She knew what it was like to have the past write hard lines into the future. She knew the pang of regret and the desire to leave things behind. And, if there was one thing she could do for him to repay his kindness so far, this was the start.

"I understand," she said. And she did.

He nodded, taking a bite of his taco and chewing thoughtfully. When he swallowed, the lightness to his words was back. "I left that all behind and decided a drastic life change was needed."

"So you became a potter."

He laughed. "It started in high school as an elective. I wasn't musical, and while I was athletic, I didn't want to take part in sports, so I tried my hand at art. I excelled when we did a unit on pottery and that came back to me after a very dark time." He glazed over it, though Charlie knew whatever had happened affected him deeply. "I poured myself into my pottery and slowly began to see that people liked it. They liked the raw aspect I gave to my pieces—a choice, mind you."

She held up her hand, fork out. "I know nothing about pottery, so I just assume everything you do is a choice."

"Smart woman." He took another bite. "Eventually, I moved here after spending a week at the Pearl Sands for vacation."

"How did you end up living on this side of the island?" The question popped out and she wondered if it had sounded insensitive, but she caught his understanding nod.

"It's real down here. I wanted that. I needed that grounding in my life when everything else was pushing me toward more—more money, more notoriety, more success. I helped Gustavo open this restaurant and got buildings made to house things we needed—the market, the small library, things like that—and started to see that my money could change people's lives. Not just mine."

Charlie smiled, and her gaze raced the lines of Nelson's face. She guessed he was close to her in age, though perhaps a few years younger. It was hard to tell, knowing that military service could age a person, but she sensed that he had seen a lot and now wanted to rest. She could resonate with that and perhaps they could find that rest together.

CHARLIE FELT FULL AND SATISFIED. Her burrito had been so large she now carried leftovers in a paper box with her while Nelson walked at her side. They adopted a leisurely pace up the beach, sand slipping between her toes. The amiable silence between them was only broken by the sound of the waves crashing to shore and retreating.

Charlie had changed the topic from their pasts to softer things—easier things—and the rest of their dinner had flown by. They talked of places they had traveled to, favorite experiences, and pastimes they both enjoyed like running and boating. Nelson made a point of suggesting they take a boat out sometime soon, and Charlie found herself agreeing, even though he hadn't mentioned inviting anyone else.

She cautioned herself to be careful. While Nelson was a kind man and obviously interested in her, she didn't want to give him the wrong impression nor did she want to move too quickly into a friendship based on the hope of something more. As much as she wanted friends, she also wanted to settle into her new job, explore the possibilities of expanding the concierge position at the Peal Sands, and adjust to life as a civilian.

It sounded silly, even in her own mind, but she saw herself as having lived such a different life up until this point that now she needed to adjust to this one. Something slower. The case that happened the very first week of starting her new job at the Pearl Sands had been a freak thing, or so she hoped, and she needed to see if she could handle the slower pace before putting down deep roots.

Though, when she looked over at Nelson walking beside her, his easy smile returning her own, and when she thought of Valentina and Stephen, she knew her heart was already involved. She'd made friends and would be hard-pressed to leave them. Hopefully, she wouldn't have to.

"What's on your schedule for the rest of this week?" Nelson asked, breaking the silence.

"The big thing was your class," she admitted. "I know Felipe wants a meeting to discuss if I thought it was 'worth it'. What do you think?"

"That sounds just like Felipe." Nelson shook his head. "I'd say the class was a success. If patrons are willing to pay for it and we have a place to set up, I see no reason we couldn't do monthly classes."

"Does that work with your schedule at *Ceramica*?" She thought of his luxury shop, knowing he usually ended up closing it if he wasn't going to be around.

"I was thinking I should hire someone full time."

"Really?" Just weeks before, he'd bemoaned the need to do something like that to her and Valentina during one of their breaks when he'd stopped by the resort. "I thought you didn't like to have to *oversee*." She used the word he had.

"I don't," he laughed. "But I can recognize when I'm being foolish, and my business would benefit from someone. And, honestly, I'm thinking of hiring someone from town."

Charlie knew he meant someone from the southern end of the island and loved that idea. "That would be a big job. Anyone you have in mind?" She hadn't met everyone who lived down there, but she had met many of them.

"I don't know that you've met her. Her name is Briana Barnson. She's an artist as well, but she works with oils and sometimes watercolor. She's very talented, but she's still young and making her way. I've thought about hiring her for a while now, but I'm worried."

"Why?"

"I don't want her to think that *I think* she belongs in a shop to manage it. I don't. I think she deserves a showing of her own, but I know that it takes time to get there. And contacts. I'm hoping that she'll get both if she manages my shop."

"That's a splendid idea." Charlie loved the sound of it and could see that he was only trying to help the young woman. "I think if you offer it to her in the right way, she's going to understand your position. Besides, she'd be helping you out."

"Maybe I will then, if you think it's a good idea. I just—" Nelson trailed off, and she followed his gaze.

Up ahead, two people were talking with the head of security, Ben Simmons. At least that's who Charlie thought it was from the distance.

"Looks like something's wrong," Nelson said.

She trusted his instincts as her own were also sensing that something might be wrong. As they drew closer, Ben shifted, and the couple came into view. "That's Monica and Will."

"The honeymooners?"

She looked up at Nelson. "How'd you know they were newlyweds?"

He laughed. "It was obvious. He couldn't take his eyes off of her."

Charlie laughed, and they doubled their speed to reach the couple and the head of security, but his confidence in the assessment of the couple gave Charlie pause. Had Nelson ever been married? It wasn't something that she needed to know, and it didn't really matter, but she was curious.

Her curiosity faded to the background as they drew near to the couple, because the look on Will's face was one of utter devastation.

"Is everything all right?" Charlie asked when they were close enough.

Ben's eyes narrowed when he saw Charlie, but the movement was so minuscule she was certain no one but her had caught it. She'd only interacted with him a few times since the first case she'd handled at the Pearl Sands. He'd been away on vacation during the investigation and only come back *after* she'd helped the police solve the crime.

He'd communicated with her in a professional manner, but she could tell he wasn't fully convinced as to her presence at the Pearl Sands. She had reminded him multiple times that she was only the concierge, yet even Felipe didn't treat her that way, and she wondered if Ben felt passed over by the resort manager.

"Charlie." Monica immediately gravitated toward her, eyes brimming with tears. "It—it's gone."

Charlie looked between Ben and Will then to Nelson before Will spoke up. "I—I mean, someone stole it. That's the only explanation."

"What's going on?" Charlie asked, directing the question to Ben.

"An item was stolen from Mr. and Mrs. Chrisman's room. I was about to go investigate."

Was it her imagination or did he seem put out to have to tell her what had transpired? "What was it?" She directed the question to Will.

At first, he looked uncertain, glancing between her and Ben, before she realized what his hesitation was. To him—and to most—she was just a concierge. Why would he tell her anything?

She was about to suggest they report the theft to the police first when Nelson spoke up. "Charlie was a private investigator before coming to the Pearl Sands. Perhaps we can help?"

Ben took in a sharp breath, and she was about to tell them they would leave the couple in the capable hands of the hotel security when Monica turned to Will. "Tell them. The more people helping the better, right?"

Will nodded. "Mon and I went out to dinner. We had reservations for seven and had a good time. We decided to come back by way of the beach. It's so nice out." He trailed off, his eyebrows furrowing as if still in shock that the item had been taken. "When we reached the beach entrance to our villa, I went in first, but right away I knew there was a problem."

"What was it that set you off?" Charlie asked out of habit.

"The sliding door wasn't locked. I *know* I locked it before we left. I mean, it's a habit, you know? But it slid right open and then when I flipped on the light, I saw that the place was a mess. Maybe not totally ransacked, but pretty roughed up. I immediately went to the place where I'd hidden the USB, but it was gone. I—I have to get it back."

Charlie noticed the hint of desperation that had come into his tone now. "May I ask what was on this USB?"

Will roughed a hand over his face. "Everything."

Frowning, Charlie looked to Monica. "Will is a well-known artist, but he's moving toward digital art and selling NFTs."

Charlie had heard the term but didn't know exactly what it meant. "I'm assuming the USB had something to do with the NFTs?"

"Something? Try everything." Will leaned closer to Charlie, his anger clear.

"Calm down," Nelson said, placing a warning hand on the young man's chest.

"Calm down? It was my life on that USB. The certificates for my NFTs are on there. That is *everything* to me."

Charlie couldn't help a stolen glance at Monica, but she only had eyes for Will.

"We'll look into this and call the police," Ben said, finally stepping into the conversation. "You can go back to your night, Ms. Davis."

Charlie felt the slight—whether unintended or not—but chose not to engage with the head of security. She tried to see things from the perspective of others, and theft on the property would land squarely in his court.

"You'd better get the police out here right now, man." Will began pacing, and Charlie took that as her cue to leave, though one last glance at Monica told her that this night —perhaps this whole trip—had not gone as planned.

4

CHARLIE'S low-heeled boots click-clacked across the highly polished floor of the resort's back hallway toward Valentina's office. She passed door after door but finally came to her friend's office and knocked.

"Come in," Valentina said, her head bent low over a report on her desk. The door was already cracked, so all Charlie had to do was push it in a little as her friend looked up.

"Charlie." Valentina's smile widened just as a black blur rocketed over her head.

Charlie flinched and barely contained a yelp as Cal the Capuchin leaped across one of the hanging walkways Valentina had installed in her office. His graceful arms swung him back and forth until he sat on a platform just behind Valentina's chair. He sat, his beady-eyed gaze leveled on Charlie as if to say, *Thank you for coming to my office.*

"I see that Cal is in a mood today," Charlie said, taking a seat across from her friend.

"He's been cooped up too much in the lobby cage. I decided to let him have a bit of freedom in the office today, but it's not quite enough."

Charlie took in the small monkey. She knew he had a penchant for stealing shiny objects and often. When something in the hotel was stolen, people came to Valentina to check if Cal had it.

Speaking of thieves... Charlie thought, winking at Cal, though the act was lost on the capuchin. "Did you hear about last night?"

"I did." Valentina shook her head. "Mr. Chrisman is so upset."

"Rightfully so, in my opinion. I don't mean anything against the security, but this hotel should be protected from thieves, and yet look what happened."

"It's shocking, to say the least. Is that why you're here?" Valentina's eyes grew wide. "You don't think Cal took the item, do you?"

Charlie laughed. "No. I mean...I don't think so."

Valentina shook her head. "I took him home last night, so I doubt he'd have been able to sneak in—although Monkey Burglar has a nice ring to it."

They laughed, but Valentina grew serious. "Are you investigating this?"

"No. Well, not exactly. Actually, I don't know."

"What does that mean?"

Charlie sighed. "I was coming back from dinner with Nelson and—"

"Wait, dinner with *Nelson*?" Valentina leaned forward, elbows on her desk. "Do tell."

"It wasn't like that. It was just…dinner with a friend, you know?"

"Mmhmm."

"Back to what I'm here to talk to you about." Charlie plunged ahead so Valentina wouldn't press further into something that wasn't important at that moment. "You'd mentioned that your brother knows who Will Chrisman is and I need to understand more about his career. I know this is short notice, but could I talk to your brother about what he knows?"

Valentina blinked. "I didn't expect that."

Charlie laughed. "I suppose I didn't really know who to talk to, but our conversation came back to me. Would that be possible?"

"Yes, of course." Valentina reached into her purse and pulled out a phone. "Let me text him to see if he's free for a call." She did and when she was done, she put the phone down to wait for his reply. "Now, tell me more about Nelson."

"Va…" Charlie rolled her eyes. "It was nothing. We went to have dinner at *La Cantina* because we were discussing how his pottery class worked. No other reason."

"Aside from the fact that you're friends." She narrowed her eyes.

"Friends. Yes."

Valentina had just opened her eyes to reply when her phone pinged. "Ah, that's Michael. Here, I'll come over there." She answered her phone in a rush of Spanish and then switched to English as she sat down beside Charlie.

"Hi, Charlie, nice to 'meet you'," he said with air quotes from the video call. "Val's told me a lot about you."

"Good things, I hope," Charlie said with a grin.

"Always," Valentina added.

"What can I help you with? Val said something about Will Chrisman?"

"Valentina said you are familiar with the art world, and I am a little confused about a conversation I had with Will last night. I'd appreciate it if this didn't get out to the public."

Most of Michael's face filled the screen, but he nodded solemnly and pulled the camera back. "I'm just at home relaxing before a shift at a local gallery I manage. I won't say a word."

"Thank you." Aside from her trust in his sister, Charlie sensed he was being genuine and forged ahead. "Last night, I came across Will and his new wife talking with the head of security here at the resort. He said a USB he'd had was stolen, and it had certificates on it or something? He also mentioned NFTs."

Michael let out a low whistle. "I hope that isn't true."

"I could have misunderstood, but I think it was."

Michael nodded slowly and looked off past the camera in a gesture she recognized as him running through the options of how things could be affected. Finally, he looked back at them.

"I was just thinking about what this may mean for him. Now, to be fair, a lot of what I've heard has been rumor and there isn't solid truth to much of it, so take that into consideration, but the word around the galleries in Florida is that Will is going fully digital."

"Art-wise?" Charlie hated how little she knew about art these days.

"Yes. There is a large market for online art, and if he mentioned NFTs, that would fall in line with what I've been hearing. Basically, some artists that started out in the physical world of art and saw success have also branched out into the digital world, but that doesn't always translate."

"I don't get it," Valentina broke in.

"If you're Michelangelo and can paint something like the Sistine Chapel that doesn't necessarily mean that you can translate that art to a digital format. And I don't just mean scanning a physical copy of the art to make it digital."

"Like you would a copier or something?" Charlie asked.

"Exactly. You have to learn a new skill to transition your art—new programs, new equipment, and new techniques."

"Sounds hard," Valentina mused.

"It is." Michael rubbed his chin, making the phone bump up and down. "But that's not the case with Will. He started out young. I think he was a teenager when he saw his first great success. A type of prodigy in the local art world. Well known enough to get into some big galleries."

"Impressive," Charlie commented.

"Yeah, well, he got bored—as I assume some kid prodigies do—and started breaking out into digital art."

"I'm guessing he was good at that too."

"No, actually. Not at first. Not up until recently. His fans thought he was trying too hard to make his digital art look like his real art, but it was failing, so he took some time off and came back with five new pieces that are honestly stunning."

"Those were, what, backed up on his USB?"

Michael laughed. "No, what it sounds like you're talking about are the certificates for his NFTs that were stored on the external drive. They are basically as valuable as the art itself."

"What is an NFT?" Valentina asked.

Charlie was glad she'd said something, or Charlie would have had to. It was a confusing concept.

"To simplify it, you're basically creating a piece of digital art and paying to certify that it is the original. That Non-Fungible Token, or NFT, identifies that art and is unique to it. You can sell it then, and it's as if you are selling that original artwork."

It was still difficult for Charlie to wrap her head around, but she was starting to understand. "If Will's NFT certificates were stolen, then it's like his art was stolen."

"In a way, yes. I still think it would be hard to sell those, but if you're talking about the art black market, then that could be different."

"At least he has his other art to fall back on, right?" Valentina said.

"Not really. I mean, again this is rumor, but I heard that he was stepping away from his contract with a well-known local gallery to exclusively do online art. All in all, it's not a super complicated process to certify art, but once it is certified, that art has a unique stamp on it. That kind of exclusivity can make the certified product worth a lot."

Charlie nodded, leaning back. It sounded like the gallery owner would have had a big reason to keep Will's digital art from being taken, but was there someone else? Someone who didn't want him to go digital, perhaps? A wild fan?

A picture of the man he'd been talking to while Monica cried came back to her. Was that man a fan?

"I've got to get ready for work, but let me know if you've got more questions. This is probably the most interesting thing I've done all month." Michael laughed, and Valentina and Charlie joined him.

"Thank you for your insight and discretion. I'll keep you posted."

They hung up, and Charlie turned to Valentina. "It sounds like there's more going on here than a simple, random theft."

"I agree," Charlie said. "And I'm going to get to the bottom of it."

———

CHARLIE WOVE through guests in the resort's elegant lobby. Dodging a bellhop, she successfully made it to the alcove where her desk was located and exhaled heavily. The conversation with Michael had enlightened her to NFTs and digital art somewhat, but she still felt like there were questions she had. The problem was she didn't know how to ask them.

Waking her computer up with a tap on the spacebar, she entered her password and drew up her schedule for the day. She'd almost forgotten the meeting she'd scheduled with Felipe to go over the first pottery class to see if he'd agree to continue hosting them. She had about fifteen minutes until he arrived, but she was mostly prepared.

She clicked open the comments document she'd downloaded the day before. She'd asked each participant to fill out a short survey on a resort iPad before they left the class. She'd heard once that if you wanted participation in something from someone, you had to give them the opportunity in person and as soon as you could or else the likelihood that they'd respond diminished by increasing numbers.

Each comment seemed better than the last. They praised not only Nelson for his easy and instructive teaching style, but also the location and equipment. Nelson had insisted on taking care of the rentals but, if she guessed correctly at the kind of man he was, she assumed he'd gone with top quality for everything. That certainly wasn't in her budget, but he hadn't complained that it exceeded the price he was being paid to teach.

She was about to print off a few pages for Felipe to take with him when a shadow fell across her desk. It was an odd sensation seeing as she was indoors and not out on the beach, but it was reminiscent of that all the same.

When she looked up, a stocky man stood over her with spiky blond hair that seemed out of place on his winkled face. He wore dark-rimmed glasses and stood with hunched shoulders.

"Hello, may I help you?"

He looked around as if he wasn't sure he was supposed to be there, though Charlie caught sight of the expensive Italian leather shoes he wore and the custom suit that fit his thin frame, so she knew he wasn't completely out of place.

She also saw how he fumbled with something in between his fingers where his hand rested at his side. She was about to ask again when a thin, hairy hand reached out from behind the man's pantlegs and snatched the gold keychain he'd been playing with.

"Cal!" Charlie leapt to her feet and raced around the desk as the monkey ducked under another desk next to hers.

"I— Wait! That's mine!" The man seemed to come to life as he whipped around to see where the capuchin had gone.

"Cal." Charlie used her stern but soft voice so as not to draw attention to the other patrons in the lobby. "Come here and give that back and I'll get you at *treat*." She said the word with emphasis and, as if by magic, the money stuck his head above the desk. "That's right. Treat time."

Charlie took her gut instinct and turned her back on Cal, despite the man's protest to her inaction—or so he thought.

"Treat," Charlie said with a singsong voice. She heard the patter of little feet just as she reached the door to his sizeable cage in the lobby. She opened the door and reached to the Cal-proof plastic box that held his treats. He leapt up next to her, resting in the open door with the key chain in one tiny hand. "Hand it over, mister." She held up the treat in one hand and offered her other for the key.

Cal considered the treat and then her open hand. One last glance at the tasty treat was all he needed to drop the keychain and reach for the treat with both of his hands.

"All right, in you go." At the familiar words, Cal jumped to the life-like branch on the opposite side of the cage and began munching while Charlie secured the door.

"Here you are, sir," she said, heading back to her desk with her hand out.

Her gaze traveled over the odd cube-shaped key chain. It looked like blocks stacked together but rested heavy in her palm like it was plated with real gold.

"Thank you," he said, snatching it from her. "Does the resort just let that monkey run around?" He sounded incredulous, but Charlie had gotten used to that response.

"We try to keep him in his cage, but he is a personal pet of one of the staff members so he occasionally slips out. On behalf of the Pearl Sands, we're sorry for the inconvenience."

He waved off her words with the flick of his finger and looked back at her desk. "Can I check in here?"

"This is actually the concierge desk, but I'm happy to check you in," she said, slipping into the chair behind her desk.

"I can go elsewhere if it's inconvenient."

"Not at all. What's your last name?"

"Vello." He spelled it out for her, and she typed it into the registration software. She didn't often check guests in, but Elijah had shown her how to help when the lines grew too long, and she was happy to do whatever she could. His name popped up on her screen. "Mr. Lucas Vello?" she confirmed.

He offered a curt nod from where he'd slid into a chair across from her.

"We have you staying for two nights, and you've requested a villa, is that correct?" It wasn't typical for guests staying for such a short time to have access to reserve a private villa, and she wondered if she'd need to call over to her front desk friend.

"Yes. I have some private business I'd like to conduct in the room, and I spoke with the manager who said that a villa would be provided. Is there an issue?"

Charlie reviewed the reservation again and saw a note area to expand which, when she clicked on it, said the same.

"I'm sorry, Mr. Vello, I didn't see the note, but it's here. We have you in Villa Amarillo. I'm sure you'll enjoy it."

"Thank you."

As she finished the check-in process, she looked over her computer at him. "You mentioned business. Is there anything that I can arrange for you, Mr. Vello? That's my job," she offered with a smile.

He looked up from his phone. "Uh, arrange? No, I don't think so."

"Very well." Charlie pulled a spare keycard from her drawer and scanned it before placing it in a narrow black folder and handing it across the desk to him. "Here is your card access to the villa. Would you like me to escort you or find a bellhop to assist you?"

"Is there a map?"

"On the lefthand side, yes."

"Then I'll be fine." He stood abruptly.

"We hope you enjoy your stay at the Pearl Sands. If there is anything we can do to make your stay more enjoyable, please let us know."

He offered a nod and gestured to one of the bellhops who had stayed by his luggage. Charlie watched him go, but her gaze stilled on another figure across the lobby. It was the man from the day before, the one who'd been watching Monica.

Charlie had the same kind of warning sensation when she saw him and, without a second thought, stood and made a beeline for him.

She wasn't sure what she was going to say when she reached him, but she needed to know if he was a guest or here for some other reason. His seeming interest in

Monica could be explained away—she was a beautiful young woman, and many men came to the resort in hopes of finding like-minded companionship. There was something about the rich that called unto other rich, or perhaps that was just her perception as someone on the outside of the dating world.

A group of five, all women in expensive workout gear with yoga matts under their arms, passed in front of her. When she looked past them, the man was gone.

Charlie moved to the spot where he'd been standing, but he'd left nothing behind. No trace or—

Her gaze stalled. She'd spun in a slow circle and her gaze landed on Monica and Will eating at one of the bistro tables. It was a precarious spot to see them, but she could just make them out from where the man had been.

Her gut told her that was no accident, but without knowing the man's name, she had no way of finding out if he were a guest or what his interest in the couple might be.

She was about to go back to her desk when Will caught sight of her and waved her over.

5

"WE WERE JUST TALKING ABOUT YOU," Will said, nudging Monica with his shoulder. "Weren't we?"

Monica nodded. "We were."

"Oh?" Charlie looked between them.

"In a way," Monica said, shifting her gaze to Will as if to gauge his reaction. "I mean, we were talking about last night—"

"The disaster," Will said, interrupting her. "Maybe nightmare is a better word choice."

"I'm assuming Security Officer Simmons was able to call the police to report the theft?"

Will's jaw clenched. "You could say that."

"Babe," Monica placed a calming hand on her husband's arm before turning to Charlie. "They did call the police, but—"

"But they sent a buffoon." Will leaned forward, pressing his palm against the table in emphasis. "This kid—and I do mean kid—knew absolutely nothing. I have no hope that he'll make a dent in my case. If there even is a case." He turned away, disgust written on his face.

"May I ask what he said? Did?"

"Are you really a P.I.?" Will said, his gaze shifting to one of calculation.

"I was—am." She shook her head. "I'm technically still licensed, but I work here at the Pearl Sands as a concierge now. I'm no longer practicing my P.I. work, but I suppose you could say I'm inquisitive?"

The corner of Will's mouth twitched. "I suppose it can't hurt. Mon?"

"He asked us the basic questions—same ones the security officer here did—and then he looked through our room and had some other guy dust for prints, but they didn't find anything. Said the lock wasn't forced and that we must have forgotten to lock it."

"Which is ridiculous," Will added. "I knew exactly what we had in that room, and I wouldn't have risked leaving it if I were going to leave the door locked."

"You didn't use the in-room safe?" Charlie asked, hoping the question couldn't set him off.

"He doesn't trust them," Monica said. "Says they are too easy to pick up and carry off—too obvious."

It seemed like an odd reason not to use the in-room safe. They were bolted to the floor as far as she knew, and to say they were obvious was perhaps true but not an adequate reason not to use the safe.

"And you didn't feel comfortable using the resort's safe? We often hold expensive artwork for our patrons who would rather keep their artwork somewhere more guarded." She asked the question tentatively, gauging whether he thought she was accusing him or not, which she wasn't. The more questions she had answers to at this point, the better.

"I asked him to," Monica said. She too looked as if she was treading lightly. "But he didn't feel comfortable with that."

"May I ask if there was a specific reason, Mr. Chrisman?"

He met her gaze as if he knew she was asking more behind her question.

"I had need of the USB and didn't want to be going back and forth. I honestly thought I'd hidden it well enough. I — Maybe that was foolish on my part."

"Is it backed up?" she asked, not knowing if such a thing were possible.

"No." Will worked his jaw again.

"I—"

"Ms. Davis."

Her name drew her attention behind them to Felipe where he stood with his hands folded, looking as if he didn't want to intrude.

"Oh, I'm sorry. Mr. and Mrs. Chrisman, this is Felipe Delgado, the hotel manager. I have a meeting I'm late for. Please, if you need anything else, I'd be happy to help you in any way I can."

"Again, Mr. Chrisman, I'm sorry for what occurred in your room last night," Felipe said. "Our best people are looking into it."

"We want her to look into it," Will said, jamming his finger toward Charlie.

She froze, her eyes going wide.

"An excellent suggestion." Felipe's smile widened. "I was going to ask her myself. Please, rest assured, we're doing everything we can to recover what was taken."

"Thank you." Will nodded and then shot a look at Charlie. "Please let me know if you have more questions. I'd be happy to answer them."

She dipped her head and followed Felipe back toward the lobby and her desk. "What was that?" she asked when they were seated.

"Despite our already-scheduled meeting, I was coming to ask if you'd look into the theft." Felipe held her gaze, and she saw the worry lines etched on his forehead. "I know I called on you last time there was something like this here at the Pearl Sands, and it was…a lot. I wasn't sure I wanted to risk asking you, but—in talking with the couple —his wife actually mentioned you by name and that you'd seen them last night."

Charlie nodded. "I ran into them on the beach speaking with Ben."

"Mrs. Chrisman mentioned that you asked smart questions and said you'd admitted to being a P.I. I thought that *was* you inserting yourself into the investigation."

Charlie's jaw dropped. "I hope you know me better than that. I wouldn't do that unless asked, and even then...." She trailed off. Nelson had been the one to bring up her former career, but he and Felipe rarely saw eye to eye on things.

Besides, did she want to get involved? She liked the couple and wanted the USB found, but was she the best person to find it?

"Charlie..." Felipe leaned forward. "I've loved everything you've brought to me. I reviewed the comments from the pottery class." At her look of surprise, he explained, "Those surveys come to my desk no matter what. But the response was overwhelmingly positive, and while I had my doubts about Nelson teaching, he seemed to be well-liked."

She almost laughed. She couldn't figure out the rivalry between the two men, but she'd picked up on it almost immediately. "Those things succeed because I'm doing my job as concierge. You have a head of security, remember?"

"I believe in you, Charlie." Felipe met her gaze, his patient and trusting. "I think you'd be able to investigate this from a trained perspective, whereas Ben might get lost in the weeds."

"What do you mean?"

Felipe frowned. "I'm not willing to get into that right now, just trust my assessment. You have the experience to look into this as well as the connection with the guests. It'll be better if you can wrap it up—and quickly." He winked, but she knew he was only half joking. The longer something like this went on, the more likely they were to get bad press for the resort, which was something they both didn't want.

"I don't think he's going to like this."

Felipe nodded. "I agree, but I'll have a talk with him. I want us to see we are all on the same team. That goes for all of the resort—waitstaff, housekeeping, front-end staff, security, the lot. We don't need to be at odds with one another."

Charlie agreed but wasn't sure putting her on this case was the way to go about it. "Maybe I should talk with Ben?"

"You have enough on your plate with hosting the next pottery class," he said with a smile.

"Really?" She'd hoped he would see the value of it, and it seemed he did.

"Really. It will be a wonderful addition, as will the other things I am sure you have percolating. And why not get that review out of the way now?"

Charlie's stomach clenched. Surely it would be good, especially if he was giving her the go-ahead to do another class. "All right."

"Do not look so worried. You have done an excellent job here so far, and I would like to push you on to the next review in three more months. At that time, you will have worked here six months, and we can decide if you would like to stay longer."

Her eyebrows rose. "Do I need to be worried?"

"I do not think so." His lips tugged into a soft smile. "The review process is for both sides, Charlie. Who is to say you won't want to go back to being a private investigator?"

She laughed. "I like this pace of life much better."

"I understand. Well, for now, focus on who might have taken Mr. Chrisman's property and report back to me."

"Alright. Are you sure about Ben?"

Despite her elation over the three-month review, Charlie wasn't sure this was the best way to foster good relationships between her and the security staff. She hadn't had to deal with this during the previous case since Ben had been away and murder was out of hotel security's boundaries, but this seemed a case for them.

"Positive. Oh, and Charlie?" Felipe held her gaze. "I'll consider adding on more staff to you when I see how things progress."

She frowned. Did he mean if she solved the mystery of the missing USB?

"Okay, Charlie?"

"I— Yes, okay." Charlie hoped she wouldn't regret this decision.

"Good." He grinned and stood.

She watched him walk away, back and shoulders straight. He was a man who got what he wanted, no matter what. Had he made a mistake insisting she work the case instead of Ben?

She pushed the thoughts out of her mind and focused on the next step of her investigation. Tonight, she'd go to Villa Blanco to investigate.

───────────

CHARLIE CHANGED into capris and a flowing blouse the color of blueberries. She pulled on a wide-brimmed hat and slipped into a pair of flipflops perfect for the beach. The weather was pleasant, perfect for an early evening stroll, especially when she was going to check out the beach access to Villa Blanco, Will and Monica's honeymoon villa.

She'd gotten their numbers from her access to their registration and sent them a text explaining that she was going to investigate as best she could into what was happening. She'd made sure to get their schedule for the night to ensure that she wouldn't interrupt them.

Taking a right outside of her cottage, she took a winding path edged with palm fronds toward the water. The sun was low on the western horizon and had left the beach in shadow, though it wasn't dark yet.

The haze that had settled in the late afternoon had thickened with an added layer of humidity. Charlie still hadn't gotten used to the weather in Florida, at least not like those born and raised there. Being from New York, it had been a shock to her system to experience her first Florida summer.

Being by the water with the stiff breeze coming off the ocean helped though, and as she stepped onto the beach, she slipped off her sandals and dug her toes into the sand. She'd never grow tired of that feeling.

A few couples and families scattered the main beach area. Some were packing up after a long day on the sand. They would no doubt go back to their rooms, change, and head to one of the restaurants for dinner. The others looked to be enjoying the evening much like herself.

Charlie was about to turn toward the path to the villas, pulling herself away from the rhythmic ocean view, when she caught sight of motion to her left. She turned halfway so as not to appear like she was staring.

It was the man from the pool. Watching Monica.

It was the same man, though it was hard to tell since he was wearing a baseball hat, but she recognized the tribal tattoo on his bicep that had been visible at the pool as well.

While it wasn't unheard of to see hotel guests in every area of the resort or in other locations on Barnabe Island, he came across as acting strangely. He didn't have the same casual air the rest of the guests put forth. He hovered near the line the palm trees created to differentiate between the resort boundary and the beach and, from where she stood, Charlie could see him looking left and right. Was he waiting for someone?

Through years of working the job as a cop in New York City as well as the rest of her time spent as a private investigator, Charlie had learned to trust her instincts. She didn't know what it was about this man that ignited her interest, but she wasn't going to ignore that.

Rather than turn toward the villas, she stayed where she was and pretended to take in the ocean while sneaking covert glances toward the man. When he turned and began walking toward the north end of the beach, she followed at a discrete distance.

He checked over his shoulder, but it was easy to tell when he was going to do that as he turned first to look up the beach before then looking back. Each time it happened, she was able to slip easily into the foliage—though anyone who might see her would think her actions strange. She only hoped no resort guests reported her to security.

When he finally stopped, they hadn't gone far. They were at the northernmost side of the beach where a row of greenery separated it from the road that led toward the entrance of the hotel. He stopped and checked his phone for the tenth time in so many minutes, and then he crossed his arms and looked out to sea.

It had only been a few minutes, and Charlie was considering just how long she'd stay out there if no one came and nothing happened, when another man appeared from the path to the beach.

It was the man she'd checked in at the concierge desk earlier that day. Lucas Vello.

While he cut a recognizable silhouette, Charlie was sure she could have picked him out in a crowd by the way he consistently fumbled with his golden block keychain.

He walked up next to the other man and the contrast was so great, Charlie had to wonder what drew them together. Where Lucas was older and hard-faced, the younger man was handsome in a model type of way.

Anyone passing by might assume they were acquaintances or perhaps just two men who'd happened to stop at the same place at the same time, but Charlie knew this meeting had been planned. Was the handsome younger man part of the business Lucas had said he was going to be conducting at the resort?

She shifted as the sun dipped lower and it became harder to see until the path lights came on and highlighted the sand with their warm glow. They gave off a magical vibe to the area, but Charlie was most thankful they would better hide her presence.

On impulse, she decided to get closer to the men to see if she could overhear something. She had to tread carefully —not only because they were guests of the resort but because Lucas had seen her and would know she was an employee.

They spoke in low tones, and she had almost gotten close enough to hear when Lucas broke off the conversation and disappeared back toward the resort.

It was abrupt, and Charlie felt the sting of disappointment. Still, she had no idea if their conversation was important or not. It likely wasn't, but she'd seen too many people lurking about the hotel recently to feel confident that something else wasn't going on.

But what?

Deciding on bold action instead of inaction, Charlie picked up her pace and approached the younger man. "Excuse me?"

He startled and turned toward her, a hard look on his symmetrical features. "Yeah?"

"I'm sorry to bother you, but do you know what time it is? I think my watch battery died." She shrugged, showing off her old-school watch and knowing he wouldn't be able to see specifics in the dim light.

"Uh, yeah." He pulled out his phone and the light illuminated his features. "Looks like it's almost seven."

"Thanks. Are you a guest here?" She was thankful she'd had time to change so she didn't look conspicuous.

"Yeah." He looked at her with suspicion.

"I mean, I know there are some pretty amazing houses up there. I was just curious. This place is incredible."

"Yeah, I guess. Um, I've got to go."

"Sure. Oh, one more thing..." She shrugged to show she was sorry to be bothering him. "I saw you talking to someone. I think I know him from somewhere, Is he... famous?" Charlie said the words with the perfect hint of adoration, as if she was just some woman fascinated by fame, but she knew she walked a narrow line. There was no evidence to say this man had anything to do with the theft of Will's USB, yet he had been caught staring at Monica as if he knew her.

It was possible he—like most of the men at the pool—had just noticed how stunningly beautiful she was. Finding out that she was a model hadn't surprised Charlie one bit. Was it possible this young man knew her though?

"Uh, I don't know. I didn't know him. He was just, um, asking me a question. You know? Kind of like you." His words were too pointed, and Charlie took that as her cue to get out.

"Got it. Well, thanks again." She waved and walked back down the beach, but her thoughts were spinning.

It was too late to go to the villa now since the Chrismans had said they were coming back from dinner at seven and she didn't want to disturb them, but that didn't mean she had to stop investigating.

Perhaps she could find a connection online, because there was no doubt in her mind that this man had met with Lucas Vello for a reason.

Why was he hiding that if there was nothing *to* hide?

6

"When you said online investigation, I thought you were joking."

Charlie looked up from her laptop at the dining room table and grinned back at Stephen Lopez where he sat next to his wife Valentina on Charlie's couch.

She remembered the day they'd gone to purchase the furniture for her small cottage and had to agree with Valentina's initial assessment that it would fit the space perfectly. It did, and it made Charlie even happier to see her two friends sitting side by side, helping her.

Well, Stephen was helping. Valentina was drinking a cup of tea and watching a reality show on the television Charlie had just purchased the week before. The volume was on low so as not to disturb them, but Charlie didn't mind. If anything, she welcomed the sound and the company.

"One of the loneliest parts of my job as a private investigator was doing research. You gave me that true crime book a few weeks back and, while I was reading it, I thought about how much research the author did. I feel it's only fair that, if you're really going to try your hand at writing true crime, you should experience your own research."

"Charlie..." Stephen shook his head. "I specifically said *fiction* crime novels."

"Don't you think that requires research too? Trust me, Stephen, I'm doing you a favor."

He grinned, shaking his head as he turned back to the computer. She knew his protest wasn't genuine—or at least not in the way it came off. He was thriving on this, and she had a feeling that if he did as well at researching and writing as he did with teaching his students in the English department at the local community college, he was going to become a great author.

A few minutes later, he snapped his fingers. "Okay, I'm seeing a connection."

Charlie put down her own notes from where she'd been researching Will's history as an artist and his move into digital art. "Let's have it."

"Oh." Valentina muted the television and turned to face them. "I'm ready."

"You shouldn't have it so easy," her husband grumbled.

"Nonsense. *I'm* not the one who said he wanted to write a book. I just like reading them—and experiencing them." She waggled her eyebrows.

A pang of regret blossomed in Charlie's chest at the thought of her sweet friend and how innocent a statement she'd made. Charlie knew Val only meant that she liked helping Charlie with a case like this, but they didn't always deal with something like theft. Like her last case, sometimes they involved murder—which meant a murderer. She didn't want to bring her friends into that, but at this point, she felt their involvement was minimal.

"Lucas Vello is the owner of an online marketplace called ArtistOcean."

"Online marketplace, what's that?" Val leaned over, but Stephen shielded his computer with a grin.

"Allow me to enlighten you."

She rolled her eyes and leaned back. "Okay, oh great researcher Stephen."

"I like the sound of that." He winked at Charlie then turned back to his computer. "It looks like ArtistOcean is a digital art gallery where you can bid on and purchase art."

"Let me guess, NFTs?" Charlie asked.

Stephen looked a little defeated. "How'd you know?"

"Michael," Val supplied.

"Oh, I didn't even think about talking with him about this," Stephen said.

"What else did you find?" Charlie asked.

"It's one of the top marketplaces for digital art at the moment and, if Reddit is to be trusted, will be the new home of Will Chrisman's work."

"Really? Did they say anything else about the deal?" Charlie knew the online forum wasn't exactly reliable news, but sometimes gossip had its roots in the truth. If what Stephen was saying was true, it could explain Vello's appearance at the resort.

"Not much. There are a few threads devoted to Will's art, and the going consensus is that he's only just come into his own."

"In what way?" Charlie asked.

"I guess his physical paintings have always been a hot commodity, but when he attempted his first showing of digital art on a high-end gallery's digital space, it flopped. You get the range of comments from every critic, naturally," Stephen explained, "but it seemed widely agreed that it was amateurish and 'grasping,' as they put it."

"Harsh," Valentina said.

"Critics usually are," Charlie mused. "But that is very interesting. Let me keep looking into Will here and then I'll share what I find."

"Perfect," Stephen said. "I'll keep looking through these forums."

They went back to work, and Charlie scoured the internet for more information on Will. While his social media seemed to be curated to focus on his newest art with only nods to his old, physical art, with no sign of the works in between that could be seen, there wasn't much that was personal on it.

Frustrated, she went back to where she'd started—his website. She'd glanced at the online gallery he'd posted, the delineation clear between digital and physical art, but this time, she kept scrolling until she reached the bottom and saw there was space for commenting enabled by a social media site.

It seemed out of place on a high-end site like this, but she began to scroll through them.

"Oh, this is interesting."

Stephen was at her shoulder in seconds with Valentina muting her show again to join him.

"I've looked through almost everything I could find for Will. There's not much going on here that you'd be surprised by. Art shows, online auctions, and lots of pictures of him at fancy places or with Monica, but then I got to the bottom and there's a comments feature."

"That seems out of place," Valentina said.

"I agree, but perhaps it's just the break we needed. Look at these comments!" Charlie ran her finger to one specifically, and Stephen read it out loud.

"'This is trash, and you know it—and I know why.' Um, that sounds borderline threating."

"It does. But since the comments are connected to social media, maybe we can find out who it is that might have motive to steal Will's art."

"If they think it's trash, why steal the art?" Valentina said.

"Let's see if Drakeinthewild has a reason." Charlie clicked on the handle, and it redirected her to a social media site. The profile picture made Charlie take a second look because she *knew* the face. "I've seen that man. *Here* at the resort!"

Both Valentina and Stephen gaped at her.

"Really?" Val asked.

"Yes. I just asked him for the time tonight, and he said he was a guest. Let's see." She looked back at the screen. "Drake Brown."

"It says he's a model," Valentina pointed out.

Charlie met her gaze. "Monica was a model, too."

"So, what, he just doesn't like Will's art because Will took his girlfriend?" Stephen asked.

"What makes you think they dated?" Valentina asked.

81

"He's got a whole album devoted to a Monica."

Charlie looked where he was pointing. She hadn't gotten that far down on the page, but there was, indeed, an album that showed Monica with hearts at both ends. He had his profile set to semi-private so she wasn't able to view the images, but when she clicked on his picture, it let her scroll through the ones he'd used for his profile.

The current image was of him alone, but the next was of him and another woman, then another of himself, then the rest were all of him and Monica in various poses. Her kissing his cheek, him with his arm around her, them on a boat on the ocean. It was clear they had been in love, or at least enjoyed each other's company.

"So this Drake guy steals the USB to get back at Will? Is that what you're thinking?" Stephen asked.

"I don't know what to think. There are still missing pieces." Charlie decided to look at Drake's header image as well, knowing that sometimes you could also scroll through that. As she did, she saw a group picture in front of what she guessed was an art gallery, if the paintings in the windows were any indication.

As she scanned the large group, things began to fall into place—though imperfectly.

"This explains some of it," she said, pointing. "There's Will and that's Monica and Drake."

"Is that an art gallery?" Stephen leaned closer to the screen.

"Oh, I know that gallery." Valentina looked between them. "You know how Michael used to manage those openings at various galleries for a while before he got his current job? He did an opening here and needed servers. This was years ago, but I helped him out for some swanky opening of some famous artist—who I didn't think was all that good."

"Do you know the name of the gallery?" Charlie asked.

"No, but I can ask Michael." She pulled out her phone and took a picture of the picture and began to text while Charlie went back to the image.

"Will's there, but not with Monica," Stephen pointed out.

"Right. I wonder if that's how she met Will in the first place."

"Kind of odd for this guy to have it in his images if that's the case, right?"

Charlie shrugged. "True, but sometimes if you change your picture, you don't think to delete the old one that's stored. Out of sight, out of mind."

"Good point."

"Okay, got the gallery name." Valentina rushed back in from where she'd stepped outside to make the call. "He says it's called Rockford Gallery owned by a Curt Mulroney, and, get this, they've hosted Will's art at that gallery *exclusively* for the last five years."

THE COTTAGE FELT empty now that Valentina and Stephen had gone home. They'd tried to dig more into the gallery, but the site was bare aside from images of the art and info about the artists.

There wasn't even information on the owner more than his name and a discrete number. Charlie felt like it was par for the course of how many high-end shops ran, but that didn't mean it wasn't frustrating.

After Valentina's fourth yawn in a row, Charlie had encouraged them to go home, promising that she'd keep them informed. Stephen looked hesitant, but she knew that he had class in the morning just as Val had work and it would do them no good to be exhausted the next day.

Charlie berated herself that she *still* hadn't seen the back entrance to Villa Blanco, but she consoled herself that the police had come and done their investigations, and that Felipe had asked her to look into what might have happened as someone with a fresh perspective, not someone who would follow in the tracks of the police.

She considered going to bed to read when a light knock sounded on her door. Startled, she looked through the side window to see Nelson.

"Good evening," he said when she opened the door.

"What are you doing here at this hour?" she asked, looking at him then behind him as if there might be another reason he'd come by.

"Just was on a walk, needed to stretch my legs, and found myself at your door." He looked up at her with a boyish grin and shrugged.

"Come on in," she said, stepping back so he could enter.

The scent of sea salt and another earthy scent she'd come to associate with him—perhaps the clay he used—followed Nelson into her small cottage. He slouched onto the couch, and she took the side chair.

"Is everything all right?"

"Yes, though I heard a rumor you're looking into the theft case for Felipe."

Charlie blinked. "How did you hear that?"

"I have my ways," he said with a grin.

She narrowed her eyes at him. There was something about Nelson she'd yet to figure out. Some way he always came by the information he did, but how? She assumed it had to do with someone—or someones—on staff, but she'd yet to prove it.

"You know I'll uncover those ways, right?"

"Challenge accepted." He leaned forward, steeping his fingers. "But really, Charlie, are you sure you want to do this?"

"Do what?" She had a feeling she knew what he meant, but she needed him to say it.

"Let Felipe manipulate you like this."

"Excuse me?" Charlie tamped down her frustration. "I'm not letting anyone manipulate me." *Including you,* she added mentally.

"Sorry, that came out the wrong way."

"Then what's the right way?"

He sighed and rubbed at the bridge of his nose. "You told me you'd come to the Pearl Sands for a new life. A change. I'm just worried that Felipe wasn't honest when he hired you and that you're finding yourself doing something you said you wanted to step away from."

Her irritation faded as she heard genuine care in his voice. "Thank you for thinking of me and caring about my situation. I have considered how I feel about all of this, but it's hard to fight one's nature."

"In what way?"

"I thought moving to Barnabe Island was going to be my retirement plan—early retirement," she added with a grin, "but I'm not sure I'm built for that. I mean, are you?"

"What do you mean?" He frowned.

"I still don't know much about your history, but it's clear you've got an investigative mind and you've found yourself helping me in the past. I don't think you'd be able to step away. I mean, isn't that why you're here now?"

The smile that overtook Nelson's face warmed Charlie at the same time it satisfied her. She was right, and he knew it.

"You *are* good, Charlene Davis."

"I think your concern is genuine, and I appreciate it, but now that we've got that out of the way, do you want to help me investigate this new case?"

He laughed, the sound resonating against her mostly bare walls. "How do you do it?"

"Do what?"

"Cut through to the heart of things like that?"

She shrugged. "It's a gift. One that—obviously—I've decided to use."

"To be clear..." He held her gaze. "I didn't want you to feel forced into any of this. I didn't want you to feel... obligated. If you want to be free from the P.I. life, you should be able to do that—no matter what's happening at the resort. And I'd stick up for you with that."

"Thank you, but I'm perfectly capable of fighting my own battles." She flashed a warm smile so he knew she wasn't offended. "But really, I do have something we can do."

"I'm at your service, ma'am," he said, doffing an invisible cap to her.

"Oh, come on," she said, shaking her head and reaching for a windbreaker.

They stepped into the night, and Charlie was glad for the slight protection against the chill. It wasn't exactly cold, and it was balmy by New York standards, but perhaps she'd adjusted better than she'd thought to weather in Florida.

She pulled out a small pocket-sized flashlight and directed them toward the beach.

"Going to tell me what we're doing?"

"Sneaking about."

His laugh was low as he followed closely. "How about a little more intel?"

"I wanted to see the back of Villa Blanco, and I didn't want to disturb the occupants before, but I'm getting impatient."

"The couple we saw on the beach yesterday?"

"Yes. I got their schedules from Monica, the wife, and I told her I'd be poking around. I wanted to go earlier, but Val and Stephen came by to help me do some reach."

"What's this? A party without me?"

"Hardly. We were on laptops all night."

"Sounds like fun," he said on a pout.

She elbowed him gently in the side. "Quiet. No need to have the other guests calling us in to Ben Simmons."

"You don't like Ben?"

She turned toward him. "I didn't say that."

"I know, but your tone said *something*."

She couldn't argue with him. "It's not a matter of dislike at all. I think he's a competent head of hotel security, but I don't think he likes me, and I feel like he'd like me even less if he found me snooping around the villas."

"Even if Felipe knew?"

She shrugged as they sidestepped through a series of lounge chairs. "Probably? I'm not sure. As the manager, Felipe can say all he wants about us being a team, but that doesn't mean everyone sees it that way."

"I can understand that. You have to *be* a team, not just talk about it."

"Exactly. I'd like to work *with* Ben, but I get the feeling he'd rather not work with me, so I let him have his space."

"I see."

They quieted as they approached the back of Villa Blanco. There were five villas all with beach-side access at the southernmost tip of the resort itself. Each villa boasted a door in the color associated with the name. White for Blanco, yellow for Amarillo, and so on.

They paused at the white gate.

"Are you going in?" he whispered.

She shook her head and began examining the gate itself. It was made of metal and hard mesh, and it connected to concrete walls that surrounded the villa to create privacy. She knew that once inside the gate, there was also thick vegetation, which she could see some of from the outside. It helped create a sense of having your own private oasis with the beach just a step away.

"I would prefer a beach view," she muttered to herself.

"What?" Nelson leaned close, and the earthy scent of him grew heavy.

"If I came here, I don't know that I'd pick a villa. I like the idea of being able to walk out my door onto the beach."

"Some want privacy."

"True. It's nice, but I'd miss the view." She thought of her own cottage. There was no view from there, but she was steps away from the beach and that was almost as good.

She turned and looked toward the end of the resort beach. "There's a camera there," she said, pointing despite the fact they wouldn't be able to see it, "but from what I've seen of those cameras, there are some obstructions to some of these villas. Still…" She walked back and forth, taking in the angle of the camera. "I feel like there should have been footage of someone coming in."

"So we're on camera right now? Do we look suspicious?"

She chuckled. "I suppose we do. But there are hundreds of cameras at this resort." She spoke more to herself than to Nelson. "Was it possible the person was just missed? But they'd have reviewed the footage."

Charlie walked toward the next villa—Roja. She had intimate knowledge of it from her last case at the resort, but nothing looked out of the ordinary. Then she moved to the villa on the opposite side—Amarillo. Careful not to shine the light in any windows, she looked between the villas. There was little space between one wall and the other.

"What are you thinking?"

"Come on," she whispered as she motioned them back toward her cottage.

"You're on to something, Charlie. What is it?" Nelson said once they were back at her cottage.

"It doesn't work, though. He only checked in today," she muttered to herself. They stepped onto the dimly illuminated path.

"What? Who checked in today?"

"Lucas Vello." She started pacing.

"Charlie." There was impatience in Nelson's tone, but she could tell he was keeping it in check.

"There are three men I've been considering while at the resort."

"Three suspects already?"

"Not exactly." She shrugged but paused long enough to let them back into her cottage. "It started with a strange man watching Monica and Will the day of the pottery class. I didn't really think much of it aside from the fact that Monica is beautiful, but then Will's USB was stolen, and that turned my focus to the strange men."

"Who are they?" he asked.

"Lucas Vello just checked in today. I checked him in, actually. Apparently, he is the owner of ArtistOcean, an—"

"Online marketplace for art. I know it."

Her eyebrows rose. Then again, he was in the art world so that made sense. "Yes. And he met with another strange man I've seen around—Drake Brown."

"Okay?"

Charlie went to her computer and pulled up the image from earlier. "I spoke with Drake, who denied knowing Lucas, and yet when we found out who he was, we could see that he'd left a very strange comment on Will's art. Plus, he was dating Monica at one point." She went on to tell him the rest of what they'd found and showed him the image.

"They are all linked somehow."

"Yes, and—" Charlie stopped as her gaze narrowed in on a man in the back row of the group photo. "That's him. The third and final 'strange man.'" She couldn't believe she hadn't seen it before, though he was partially hidden at the back.

"Who is he?" Nelson asked.

"I have no clue, but..." She hovered her mouse over the image and a name popped up. "Curt Mulroney. Well, that makes sense."

"What makes sense?" Nelson looked between her and the photo.

"He owns the Rockford Gallery."

7

CHARLIE'S KNEE jumped up and down as she sat at her desk. She'd set up a time to meet with Will and Monica, and she still had fifteen minutes before she could leave—though she'd still be early at that point.

She was anxious to get all of her questions out. She also wondered how her questions would be taken. Would Will feel attacked if she started digging into his past? Was it possible the gallery owner where his art was exclusively exhibited had a meeting with him, which was why he'd come to the Pearl Sands?

Charlie didn't like coincidences though, and it seemed improbable that Curt, Lucas, and Drake had all arrived at the same resort without Will knowing about it.

And what about Monica? What was her role in all of this? She'd appeared unconnected until Charlie saw the host of pictures she had with Drake Brown.

Giving up on being productive at her desk, Charlie stood to leave for the Seaside Café, but she jumped when Juliana appeared before her.

"I am sorry to have startled you," the young woman said. She was dressed in everyday clothes, and Charlie assumed she'd either just gotten off a shift or was heading to one.

"It's okay, Juliana. I didn't see you come up."

"Is it a bad time?" She bit her lip nervously, and Charlie slowed her racing thoughts to focus in on the woman. Juliana twisted her purse strap in her hands and shifted from one foot to another. She was nervous.

"Not at all. I have a meeting soon but have a seat." Charlie came around her desk and sat facing the woman. "What is it?'

"I…" Juliana licked her lips. "I know this is maybe not be the proper time, but I was wondering if perhaps, maybe…." Juliana met Charlie's gaze and then looked down at her hands.

"What is it, Juliana? You can tell me anything. Goodness, without you on my first day of work, I might have run away scared from this whole place."

"What? Really?"

Charlie laughed. "You were the first person to be nice to me and that boosted my confidence so much. How can I help you?"

Seemingly bolstered by Charlie's words, Juliana took a deep breath. "I overheard Valentina talking to one of the other maids about how you were considering growing the concierge desk program. That you were looking to hire someone and… I know you do not know much about me or my background, but I am very capable, and I love to learn, and—" She stopped as if realizing she was rambling. "I would like to be considered for the position."

Charlie's eyebrows rose. She and Felipe had talked about creating more opportunities at the resort for people to register for courses and excursions and to create a more-personal experience for each guest, but Charlie knew it would take time to grow that and find the right people to fit into those positions.

Still, there was an open honesty about Juliana that Charlie had liked from the beginning.

"I don't know that I have any authority to hire or even consider anyone at this point," she said, and the woman looked crestfallen. "However, I will certainly take your request into consideration. I think you could be a valuable asset, I just don't know what that will look like yet."

"I understand. I did not think it would be right away," she said. Her Spanish accent softened her words, but she smiled with more confidence.

"Good. Thank you for coming to me. It took courage, I'm sure."

She dipped her head. "You are a very kind woman, but it is always hard to ask for something. I have worked here for almost six years now, and while I have enjoyed my time in housekeeping, I have a degree in hospitality and would like to put it to use."

"You do?"

Juliana nodded. "It is from an international school though, and I had trouble finding work before I received my green card. I think I was too afraid to risk my current job to aspire to anything else." She shook her head. "I thought— if I do not try, I will never know."

Charlie reached out and gripped the woman's hand for a moment. Just enough to comfort her before she pulled away. "I appreciate your boldness and your bravery. It may take some time, but I'll see what I can do."

Juliana nodded and stood. "Time for my shift. Thank you, Ms. Davis."

"Charlie," she enforced. "Please."

"Thank you, Charlie." The woman dipped her head and left through the service entrance that led toward the housekeeping lockers. Charlie checked her watch.

It was time to leave for her meeting, but she was still stuck on the fact that Juliana had a degree in hospitality— more than Charlie could boast—and yet she was working as a maid. There was nothing wrong with being a maid, of course, but Juliana was overqualified for the role.

Charlie set her mind do something about it, but she had to get to her meeting right then.

The scents of coffee and sea salt grew strong as Charlie neared the Seaside Café. It was her favorite little hideaway and serviced those spending time on the beach. The floor-to-ceiling glass doors slipped into the wall to open the space up for an indoor-outdoor feeling, though they could be closed in the cooler months while preserving the natural light.

Charlie chose a dark chocolate mocha this time, opting for something a little richer than she normally would have, and selected a seat in the shade on the patio.

She sipped the bittersweet brew and took in the scene. Families and groups of people played volleyball on the sandpit courts, women and men sunbathed in the provided chairs with blue-and-white-striped cushions, waiters carried out iced drinks from the snack and drink kiosk closer to the water, and some of the older resort guests walked slowly along the shore.

It was the perfect day with bright sun and a cool breeze that wasn't too stiff. For the first time since she'd started working at the Pearl Sands, Charlie wished she had the day off to roam and enjoy the beauty of Florida in April.

She'd had plenty of time off, but up until now, she'd spent most of it adjusting to her new life. Figuring out the best places to shop for groceries that weren't too far, shopping to outfit her small cottage, and spending time with her new friends.

Settling in was something that took time, Charlie knew that, but adjusting to the beauty of Pearl Sands was going to be a bit more difficult.

"You look lost in thought." Monica slid into the seat in front of Charlie.

"I'm sorry. I think I was." Charlie laughed. "You already got your drink and everything." She eyed the cup and then looked back to search for Will.

"Will had a call he had to take. He should be here soon—I hope." Monica covered her lackluster smile with a sip from her coffee.

Charlie schooled her features at the news of Will's absence. He was the one she really needed to talk to, and yet it would be good to talk to Monica on her own as well.

"I was just thinking how it's an adjustment to live here," Charlie said.

"I'm sure. I can't imagine living in a place like this. It'd be like vacation all the time."

Charlie laughed. "Until you work in the service industry."

"I've been there. I know how it is." Monica dropped her gaze. "I was a waitress for a long time before my career took off."

"You mean, as a model?"

"Yeah." She turned her gaze toward the ocean. "I was scouted. I mean, who thinks that stuff happens in real life, you know? But it did. I didn't quit my day job, though. Not at first."

Charlie nodded. "I assume things went well?"

"Really well." A pink blush tinted her cheeks. "I think it was when I was in Milan that it hit me—I'd made it. I never went back to waitressing and…here I am."

"You said you do graphic design now, though?"

"I do." A far-off look entered her eyes. "It was about four years ago that I started taking classes. I'd gotten in a car accident and, while I wasn't badly injured, I couldn't work for a while. It got me thinking—my looks aren't going to last forever. I need something else."

"Is that how you met Will? Through your classes?"

Monica laughed. "No." She winkled her nose. "I was actually at a gallery opening where I met him. But I was dating someone else."

Charlie's stomach clenched. It had to be Drake. "What happened there?"

"The guy I was with… He's a great guy, but there was something about Will that drew me. He's funny and sweet, but he's brilliant. His art is just…amazing. And he started telling me all about it, and I could see his passion for it. My ex… Well, let's just say he didn't have many aspirations."

"What happened between you two?"

Monica's brow furrowed. "Why do you ask?"

Charlie took a breath and thought of how best to approach her questions. "I didn't realize how much adjustment it would take me to get used to life on Barnabe Island. What I didn't realize was that it wasn't the setting so much as the work. I've been an investigator for most of my life and coming here... I couldn't set that aside. I ask about your ex because, if I'm going to investigate the theft of Will's flash drive, I have to look at all aspects. I can't get lost on the beach; I have to come into the cold reality of who people are, if that makes sense."

Monica nodded slowly. "He's here."

Charlie leaned forward. "What?"

"Drake. He's here at the resort." She flashed at look at Charlie. "But he wouldn't do anything like what you're talking about. He couldn't." Was that hesitation Charlie saw?

"Sometimes we don't know what our loved ones—or former loved ones—are capable of."

"But Drake... I think he's just trying to get back at me."

"Why do you say that?"

"I saw him with some beautiful woman—probably another model. I hate to say it, but I don't think he's over me. I met Will about eight months ago, while I was still dating Drake, but I broke things off with Drake right away. Will and I got engaged about two months ago, and...now we're married. Drake just needs to get over it and accept that."

"If he's the type of man who would try to make you jealous, is he also the type of man that would try to get back at you for something?"

"Like stealing Will's art?" Her shoulders sagged. "I— I don't think so."

Charlie wasn't confident in her assertion of Drake's innocence, but she let it go and switched topics. "Can you tell me more about the art on the USB and why Will has it with him on his honeymoon?"

Monica's gaze snagged on something at the beach, and she stood abruptly. "I— I don't know. I really don't. I'm sorry, but I have to go." She met Charlie's gaze, and Charlie saw the pain in her eyes. "I'm not feeling well."

"Can I—" Charlie started to offer to help, but Monica spun and left, her drink forgotten.

When Charlie turned to see what Monica had seen, she caught sight of Drake with a woman wearing a bikini. They were laughing as he grabbed her and pulled her close, kissing her deeply.

Monica was married to Will and said that Drake needed to move on, but did she need to do the same?

CHARLIE WATCHED Monica weave through the line of people waiting to order coffee drinks. She shifted her attention back to the beach and this time, Drake's gaze followed Monica as she took the path back toward the main area of the resort.

Had he positioned himself and his new girlfriend in view of Monica because he'd followed her to their meeting? It seemed unlikely, though the timing was odd.

Tossing her empty cup in the trash, Charlie decided to take a circuitous route back to the lobby. The path took her by the beach, and she watched Drake through the leaves of bushes that separated the path from the sand.

While he'd appeared distracted by Monica, he hadn't left to follow her. Charlie counted that as a good sign. She took another path under the branches of tall palm trees, smiling at several guests she passed, but halted when she caught sight of Monica.

Charlie had expected her to be back at the pool to meet up with Will, but she sat on a stone bench, huddled over her phone. It was a sad sight, a young woman on her honeymoon without her husband and facing the specter of her past with her ex-boyfriend coming to the same resort. She seemed sweet and ambitious, but there was an air of confusion about her.

Did Monica still care about Drake enough that his presence could affect her? Or did the difficulty stem from remembering how she'd met Will and left Drake in the process?

Charlie was about to enter the staff hallway and leave Monica to her private moment when movement across the courtyard caught her attention. Curt Mulroney stood partially hidden by a colonnade, watching Monica.

Charlie wasn't surprised she recognized him, seeing as he looked nearly identical to his photo on Drake's social media header, but to see him watching Monica made Charlie uneasy.

Bypassing the staff hall, Charlie took the path around to the opposite end of the courtyard and boldly walked up to Curt.

"Hello," she said, startling him out of his focused attention on Monica.

"I— Hello." Dressed in faded blue slacks and a white button-up that had seen one too many washes, he wore a pained expression and cast another glance toward Monica. Thankfully, they were far enough away that she wouldn't hear them unless their conversation resorted to shouting, which Charlie didn't anticipate.

"Can I help you find something?"

"Find— Uh, no. Thank you." His gaze flickered to the Pearl Sands logo on her white polo before he put on a fake smile. "Just enjoying the weather."

It was a ridiculous thing to say, and Charlie was certain they both knew it. She weighed her options: leave and let him continue his watch or confront him. Charlie had never been good at subtlety.

"Why are you watching Monica?"

He jolted upright from where he'd leaned against the column, no doubt trying to look relaxed.

"And have you been following her?"

"I— What? No. I..." He looked back at Monica. "I'm not."

"You are." She held his gaze. "I've seen you near her multiple times."

"Who are you?"

"I work for the resort." She didn't feel the need to clarify anything more.

"It's none of your business what I do." He leaned closer, as if trying to intimidate her.

"But it is. I'm in charge of the well-being of guests at this resort and I—*the resort*—won't stand for stalkers on its premises."

He huffed out a breath. "I'm not a stalker. I promise." She saw the moment he decided to explain. "I know Monica's husband Will and have been trying to speak with him alone. That's been a surprisingly difficult task."

"Does he want to speak with you?"

Curt opened his mouth then closed it. His gaze shifted back to the courtyard, but while they'd been speaking, Monica had left. Charlie caught Monica's movement and had angled herself in such a way that Curt had to turn toward her, effectively cutting off his view of her.

"Rats. She's gone," he said through clenched teeth.

"Sir, I need to know if it's necessary for me to call in hotel security. We can't have guests stalking other guests."

"I'm not stalking anyone," he said, his voice raised. He seemed to sense he'd neared a line and took a step back. "I'm not. It's just about business."

"While he's on his honeymoon?"

Curt gave her an odd look. "Nothing has ever stopped Will from conducting business—not even the death of his mother." He seemed serious about this, but he could have easily been exaggerating.

"Sir," she began again, wanting to try yet again to get him to explain *why* he needed to speak with Will, but he stepped back. He looked over her shoulder, shook his head, and muttered an oath.

"It's nothing you have to worry about," he said before stepping around her and stalking off down the hallway.

She turned and, to her surprise, saw Drake standing at the end of the outdoor corridor. He wore no shirt and sunglasses on the top of his head and stared directly at Curt. She watched as the gallery owner drew near, and everything about Drake's posture changed. He fisted his hands, making the tanned muscles of his forearms shift, and wrinkles appeared on his forehead.

It was clear to Charlie that they were arguing, but she had no idea what it was about. As if sensing her gaze, Curt turned around and looked back at her before lightly touching Drake's arm and pointing down the hallway away from Charlie.

Drake shook off his touch but turned to follow him.

As Charlie watched the two, she got the distinct feeling they not only knew one another but had important things to discuss.

Things she wished she were privy to.

Her mind immediately went to the stolen USB. Had Drake taken it to get back at Monica? Was Curt in on the whole thing and trying to get it from him? Without any evidence but association connecting the two, there was no way to dig deeper on that, though she hoped the police were doing a deep dive into Will's business connections.

Charlie looked back to the courtyard. Was Monica aware of any of this? Of her ex-boyfriend's connection to her new husband's gallery owner? And had Curt told the truth about wanting to speak to Will?

It seemed obvious that Will would talk to the gallery owner where his art was exhibited, yet Curt acted like Will was ignoring him or unwilling to talk to him.

"Or is this not about Will at all?" Charlie spoke the words to the cool breeze that rushed in from across the beach.

She'd seen Curt looking at both Will and Monica, but today, he was watching Monica. Was he really just looking for an opportunity to speak with Will, or one to talk with Monica?

Charlie's phone buzzed in her pocket, and she looked down to see a text from Elijah about guests needing her services. She'd been away from her desk long enough for one day.

Shoving aside the puzzle of Will, Curt, Drake, and Monica, she turned back to the staff hallway and swiped her card to enter. It was cooler inside, and she suppressed a chill. There were no leads on the USB, but plenty of people that cared about Will's art. Which one had decided it was time to take what they wanted?

CHARLIE RAISED her arms over her head and stretched out the stiffness in her neck from the impromptu nap she'd taken on the couch after her shift ended. In between assisting guests and setting up schedules for new guests arriving in the coming weeks, she'd puzzled over the USB problem.

She'd wanted to get into the villa to see exactly where Will had hidden it and how likely it would be that someone would come across it in a random search, but her calls to Will and Monica had both gone unanswered throughout the day.

It was odd. For a man who'd seemed very invested in finding his USB and insistent that she help them, she thought he would have been more willing to return her calls—especially after she left a text and voicemail detailing exactly what she wanted to discuss with him.

Coming back to the cottage to change and grab a snack, Charlie had settled on the couch with her computer. She'd searched online for more information about Will, Curt, and even Lucas Vello, but there was very little of what she'd call "real" news. Plenty of gossip sites talked about rumors, or rumors of rumors, but that wasn't solid evidence.

One site seemed to confirm what Michael had said, explaining that after several rough years of creating digital art, Will had finally found his place. The article had gone into detail about his earlier works of art and how they'd come across as inspired. The article had claimed that it was unheard of for someone so young to paint with such feeling.

From what Charlie could gather, Will had been something of a savant. Then he'd switched to digital art, seemingly without any plans to continue his oil paintings. But why?

Charlie paced across the small, combined living and dining room areas, puzzling it out. She needed to talk to Will about his past. Something as personal as a USB with NFT credentials on it wasn't a typical thieves target.

And why the switch to digital when it was clear his physical art was selling well? According to another article Charlie had read, Will could have been world renowned if he'd continued on the path of oil paintings, but they'd stopped abruptly five years before.

Her stomach grumbled, and she turned to look at the small kitchen. Her cupboards were sadly bare, and she knew she'd only find a head of lettuce and a stick of butter in the refrigerator. Perhaps tonight was a night to treat herself to the delicious, authentic Mexican food at *La Cantina*.

Pulling on a light sweatshirt and slipping into boat shoes, Charlie stuck her phone in her back pocket and placed her keys and cash in the front. She stepped outside, locked the door, and turned toward the resort.

She wasn't sure of the young woman's schedule, but Juliana's request came to mind and Charlie wondered if she was around to join her for a quick meal. The idea of bringing Juliana on to the concierge team was appealing, but she wanted to get to know more about the woman first. It was possible that she'd seen this as a step up, but what if she were ready for even higher management? Charlie wasn't going to let her step into a job she was over-qualified for—again.

When she reached the staff lounge, Charlie stepped to the computer terminal and typed in her employee ID. It gave her access to the daily schedule, and she searched the housekeeping staff for Juliana's name.

"Perfect." The woman's shift was ending in fifteen minutes.

Charlie texted Valentina and asked where Juliana might be working at that moment and got a quick reply that she'd be restocking the cart for the next shift.

The ins and outs of a large resort still eluded Charlie after several months of working at the Pearl Sands, but she'd learned quickly that a hotel never truly sleeps. There are always things to be done, though many of them happened behind the scenes at night.

She found the housekeeping area that Valentina suggested she check first and, to her delight, saw the woman there with one earbud in, folding towels and placing them in a nearly fully-stocked cart.

"Juliana?"

The woman's hands stilled on the towel she was reaching for as she turned around. Her surprise soon turned into a smile. "Charlie, what are you doing here? Did you need something from housekeeping?"

While Charlie didn't have maid service, she'd needed a few toiletries her first few weeks at the resort. Juliana had helped her each time.

"No, and I'm sorry to bother you. I know your shift is almost over. I was wondering if you had time to go to dinner with me at *La Cantina* once you're done?"

"At the south end?" The woman looked surprised that Charlie would suggest the local restaurant.

"Yes, that's the one."

"I— I'd love to. Are you sure you want me to go with you?"

Charlie laughed. "Of course. Why wouldn't I?"

"I didn't really bring *nice* clothes." She was in her maid uniform, but Charlie assumed she'd brought something to change into. All the maids did.

"It doesn't matter to me what you wear. I just wanted to have a conversation with you about what we talked about before. Unofficially, of course."

Hope brightened her eyes and she nodded. "Then yes. If you can wait another ten minutes or so, I can finish up here and change."

"No rush. I'll wait for you in the staff lounge."

Julianna nodded, and Charlie saw her pick up the pace of her folding as Charlie left for the lounge. It was a comfortable area with seating, a ping-pong table, a small kitchen with a refrigerator, a pantry, and a television that always seemed to be turned to some sports game or another.

Charlie didn't spend much time in here, preferring to take walks on her breaks or slip back to her cottage for lunch, but the few times she'd been in here, the atmosphere was relaxed and cheerful.

Tonight was no different. Maintenance staff, waiters, and even one of the front desk assistants were there relaxing in chairs. A few watched the game, and the rest chatted or looked at their phones.

Charlie took a seat and pulled up the reading app on her phone. She was only a few pages in when Juliana appeared at her side. She wore dark jeans and a t-shirt with a light sweater over the top. While Charlie didn't say anything so as not to make the woman uncomfortable, she thought she looked perfectly fine and wasn't sure what her worry had been.

"Ready?"

Juliana nodded, and they left the lounge as the woman waved farewell to a few of the other maids.

"I'm nervous," she admitted as they walked through the wide hallway that ran alongside the first pool.

"Don't be," Charlie said with a grin. "Think of this as dinner with a friend. We may talk about work, but not exclusively. I'd like to get to know you."

"I like the sound of that."

Night had fallen, and the sounds of laughter at the swim-up bar in between the pools overpowered everything else. Lights glowed along the walkway, and the breeze brought a salty flavor with it.

They passed the second pool and made it out onto the walkway that led past the Seaview Café and toward the southernmost part of the resort. They'd have to either walk along the beach or take the road to *La Cantina,* but there would be enough light. Charlie knew this from past experiences.

They had just made it to where the path split to a Y when a scream shattered the quiet of the night.

Juliana jumped. "What was that?"

"I-I don't know?" Charlie turned in a circle and looked around.

No one was close to them but, down by the water, she saw a crowd starting to form. Another scream pushed her into action.

Without thinking, she rushed toward the crowd, Juliana a few steps behind her. They skidded to a stop at the edge of the crowd, and Charlie used the voice she'd honed as a cop so many years before.

"Move aside. Resort staff."

The men and women parted, and she got her first look at what had caused the scream.

Drake Brown lay on the sand—shirtless, tanned, and dead.

8

I t was hard to tell in the dim light, but Charlie knew from experience that he was no longer with them. It didn't stop her from rushing forward to check his pulse.

"Someone call 9-1-1. Right now," Charlie shouted. No one moved. She looked up and saw Monica staring in shock. "Monica. Call 9-1-1. Now!"

Her name seemed to jolt her into motion, and she pulled out her phone as Charlie shifted back to Drake. She didn't touch him, aside from checking for his pulse, because she knew what this was.

A crime scene.

"Everyone step back." She channeled her inner sergeant. "Do it now."

They did, but a few lingered. Juliana was one of them. "What can I do, Charlie?"

"Go to the hotel and get security. Tell them we've called the police. Make sure someone knows to direct everyone here." Charlie shrugged. "And sorry, but it looks like we'll need to reschedule dinner."

She nodded. "Not a problem." Then, without hesitation, Juliana rushed back to the resort.

Charlie turned back to the body. Drake had no shirt on and wore a pair of swimming trunks. There were no sandals on his feet, and his hair was wet as if he'd been in the water a short while before. Had he drowned?

There was something in the back of her mind that was picking up on something, though, even if it was subconsciously.

Charlie sensed movement and looked up to see Monica. "What happened?"

"I don't know." Monica blinked, her gaze fixed on Drake. "I was just taking a walk to clear my head when I came across…"

She didn't have to finish her sentence. Charlie looked back down at the body, and that was when she caught what she'd missed before. As Monica had stepped closer, the flashlight on her phone illuminating the area better, Charlie saw what her brain had already seen: marks on Drake's neck.

"Come on." Charlie put an arm out and pulled Monica back from the body. "We'll wait over here."

"But…Drake." Monica seemed at a loss for words.

"He's gone." Charlie softened her voice as best she could. "Let's leave the body for the police. Everyone!" Charlie looked around the circle. "Step back. The police are on their way."

Monica nodded. As they stepped back, Charlie watched the surf to make sure it wouldn't reach Drake and erase vital evidence. It appeared to have reached full tide, and she felt herself relax somewhat. It wouldn't come closer. She didn't want to contaminate a crime scene by moving the body if she didn't have to.

Charlie shifted her focus to the woman standing next to her. Monica's phone flashlight was still on, and Charlie noticed the woman's hands for the first time. They were covered in clay.

Charlie was about to ask what she'd been doing that night when the sounds of male voices drew her attention. It was hotel security.

They rushed to the scene, and Charlie saw Ben catch sight of the body on the beach. His jaw tightened and he seemed to steel himself before barking orders to his men to keep everyone back.

Charlie left Monica to approach Ben. Something shifted behind his eyes as she approached, but she chose to ignore it, going for an informational approach. "I was with Juliana Gomez walking to the southern part of the island to have dinner when we heard screams. Came to the beach and found…this."

She watched his face for indications that he felt overwhelmed by the task of finding yet another body at Pearl Sands, but the man gave nothing away.

"Got it. The police are en route. Should be here in minutes. I'm sure they'll want to interview you."

She nodded. "Naturally. And everyone else."

He caught her meaning and barked an order to a young man with blond hair wearing a black polo. Ben made sure he knew he needed to keep everyone near and then turned back to her.

"How is it you're always around when bad things happen?"

Charlie wanted to laugh but saw the seriousness of his question. She knew it wasn't funny—murder never was—but it did seem to be her luck that she was near when bad things happened.

"I don't know, Mr. Simmons, but I will say that I don't like it."

His eyes narrowed and he turned back to the man. "Do you know this guest?"

She tried to gauge the reasoning for his question but decided to answer honestly. "Yes and no. I wouldn't say I *knew* him, but I have spoken to him once. He's the ex-boyfriend of that woman over there." She pointed to Monica.

"Did she find the body?"

"Unclear. It sounds like there were others on the beach and she happened upon them, but the police will have to connect the stories to know what is true."

He nodded once as if he'd thought the same thing. "Do you think this has anything to do with the theft a few days ago?"

His question wasn't out of the blue, but it caught her off guard all the same. Perhaps the shock of seeing a dead body—yet again—had fogged her mind, but the connections began coming together. Monica had chosen Will over Drake. Drake had spoken to Curt, the owner of the gallery where Will's art was being sold. The art that Will would no longer be making.

Then there was Lucas Vello, who'd spoken to Drake as well that night on the beach. Drake seemed to be integral to whatever was going on with Will and his art, but in what capacity? And who would have had motive to kill him?

She'd thought all of this in the span of a few seconds but decided to ask a question herself. "Did you notice the ligature marks, too?"

He turned toward her. "I did."

"I would say that there must be a connection, and that's part gut, part investigation-based."

He nodded once. "Keep me in the loop."

With that, he walked away, helping his men corral the growing crowd and trying to keep the original group of people who had found Drake separate so that the police could question them.

Charlie wasn't sure what to think of Ben. Was he an ally? And enemy? Though that word was dramatic and too far from reality, she thought he could become one if he felt she was stepping on his toes. It all depended on what type of man he was.

She wrapped her arms around herself as flashing lights appeared in the distance on the beach. The police were coming.

They rode up in squad cars with an unmarked car following. Immediately, a swath of blue uniforms filed out and stepped in to take over for the hotel security. They established a perimeter, and a young officer with thin posts and caution tape erected a safe area around the body.

Charlie watched it all as if in a daze. This was her past. Same procedures, different location. A similar scene played in her mind. She was in Central Park where someone had been murdered and the crime scene tape had just been set up when she arrived.

She was so lost in thought she almost missed the arrival, but something in the atmosphere yanked her back from the past and landed her solidly in the present just as a voice began barking orders.

A woman stepped onto the scene illuminated by the cars' headlights. She was a few inches taller than Charlie with dark brown hair streaked with gray pulled back into a ponytail. She wore a blazer and slacks over sensible black shoes and had a gun at her hip, badge hanging around her neck from a metal chain.

Charlie categorized those things in seconds, but the moment the woman's eyes hit hers was when she knew.

This was the new detective, and she was going to be a force to reckon with.

CHARLIE WATCHED from her place behind the caution tape as officers began to interview witnesses. Monica was crying now, and Charlie saw her pulled aside by an officer she recognized. Pearson, she thought his last name was. He had worked closely with the last detective that had come to the Pearl Sands. Don had been on his way to retirement when he caught the case at the resort and had worked closely with Charlie until the killer was apprehended.

Now, as Charlie observed the new detective take charge of the scene, she had a feeling things would be different. It wasn't that she wanted to insert herself into the investigation, but there had been plenty of times in the past when her insight as a private investigator had been crucial to solving a case.

P.I.'s had a bad rap sometimes. They were often looked at as failed detectives or money-grabbing, but she'd been neither of those things. She'd been sure she would have made detective in New York, but it would have taken too long, and her younger self hadn't wanted to wait.

That was Charlie though, charging ahead without thinking everything through. She often wondered what might have happened had she stayed and worked her way up in New York. Then again, she wouldn't trade her life in Florida for anything—not even regrets from the past.

The detective slipped under the crime scene tape, pulling on plastic gloves, and began to examine the body. Charlie edged closer to the side. Was it possible that this woman, like Detective Don Neal, would be receptive to outside observation?

Charlie doubted it, but she had to try. Finding a dead body was yet another shocking thing to happen at the Peal Sands, and Charlie was certain Felipe would ask her to look into it. And, like she'd discussed with Nelson, she was all right with that. Still, cooperation with the police meant she had to be on friendly terms with them to do so.

"Did you notice the strangulation marks on his neck?"

The woman's head snapped up and her eyes lasered in on Charlie. "What did you say?"

"Hi, I'm Charlie Davis. I work at the Pearl Sands and—"

"I asked what you said." The woman's reply was barked much like an order.

"Strangulation marks. On his neck. I noticed them when I checked his vitals."

Her eyes narrowed. "I'm going to say this one time, and one time only. This is a *crime scene*. You need to back up, ma'am."

Charlie felt her ire rise, but she tamped it down. "I am a fully licensed private investigator, and—"

"And nothing. That means *nothing* to me. I don't know you. You're just some random woman telling me about a dead body. If anything, you're a suspect."

"Throwing out accusations, are we, Sophia?"

Both women turned to see Nelson there, his hands in the pockets of his linen pants. "What are you doing here, Hall?"

Charlie blinked. She knew Nelson?

"I live here. This is basically my beach," he added with a grin. "But I also think you're being a little harsh. Charlie is the one who helped Don during the last murder investigation here at the Sands."

The detective—Sophia—barked a humorless laugh. "Right. And that's supposed to, what? Make me sympathetic? I don't care who she is. She's at a crime scene, and I have work to do."

"Good thing you didn't become a doctor, you have no bedside manner." Nelson shook his head.

Charlie turned toward the detective, sure she was going to chew him out further, but her features softened. "Yeah, I'm definitely not doctor material. Now take your lady-friend here and step away from my crime scene." She shifted her gaze to Charlie. Was it just the light or did Charlie see a miniscule of reassessment there? "I need to check out these strangulation marks."

Nelson placed a gentle hand on Charlie's arm, but she moved out of his touch. Despite the fact that he'd somewhat eased the tension between her and the new detective, she didn't like having to rely on that. She wanted to stand on her own two feet, not be handed a connection with a tough woman who only needed to come around in her understanding of who Charlie was.

The minute those thoughts entered her mind, Charlie felt ashamed. Of *course* she could benefit from a personal introduction to the hard woman. That was how a lot of these things worked. In fairness to Sophia, she knew nothing about Charlie, and Nelson had given her a window into who she was based on his own experience. That seemed to go somewhere with the woman—even if that wasn't very far.

"Thanks," she said, once they'd stepped back to where the crowd was gathered.

"Detective Sophia Perez is a tough cookie. I mean that with all respect to her and her profession. She hasn't made it as far as she has without being…"

He searched for the word, and Charlie supplied it. "Focused?"

"I was thinking, hard." He grinned. "But that sounds better. She's good at what she does, but she attacks things like a bulldozer and will run over anything she has to in order to close a case."

Including people. "I got that feeling," Charlie said. "How do you know her?"

"We go way back." Nelson didn't add anything further, which only fueled Charlie's curiosity, but she held it back. Now was not the time to dive into personal history.

Her gaze traveled the crowd, as she knew some of the officers would be doing as well. You never knew who would be among the observers. While the crowd was by no means large, it held enough people that someone could be looking on with ill intent among the naturally curious.

When she spotted Monica, now joined by Will, in a private area held by Officer Pearson, she made a snap decision.

"I'm going to do something I don't think Detective Perez will approve of."

Nelson's eyebrows rose. "Do tell."

"Follow me." She wove through the people, the scent of faded sunscreen and alcohol mingling among them as they stood illuminated by the headlights of the police cars.

A few asked one another what had happened, and Charlie caught sight of more onlookers coming from the resort, but they would be stopped by the officers—or possibly hotel security—before they reached this part of the beach.

DANIELLE COLLINS & MILLIE BRIGGS

"It's Officer Pearson, right?" She said, stepping up behind the younger man. He was only a few inches taller than Charlie and built like a body builder beneath his dark uniform. His tan, even darker than when she'd seen him before, made his white teeth stand out like they were illuminated by a blacklight.

"Yeah, you got it." He nodded once, head tilting to the side. "Charlie?"

"You remember." She pushed her smile wider. "If I remember, Don was what? Mentoring you? You're going to be a detective, right?"

He dropped his gaze, thumb going to his utility belt in an obvious show of affected humility. "Yes, ma'am. That's the goal, at least."

"That's incredible. I remember back in my rookie days—"

"You were a cop?" His eyebrows rose.

"Didn't Don tell you? I was one of New York's finest." She didn't need to say more, she saw the awe reflected in his eyes.

"That's incredible."

"Part of the job. But you know that."

He dipped his head. "I do. And here we are, out at the Sands again. Can't believe it, to be honest."

She looked over his shoulder at Will and Monica. "Are they in custody or something?"

"Or something? Detective Perez—she's who took over for Don—she said I needed to keep an eye on them."

"Got it." She feigned hesitation. "Do you think I could talk to them? It's just that they are honeymooners, and this is their first time at the resort. I want to assure them that things will be okay. That this doesn't always happen here." She added a humorless laugh.

"I— I mean, I guess it couldn't hurt."

Charlie felt more than heard Nelson hold in a laugh behind her. She'd almost forgotten he was there, but her focus was on speaking to Monica.

"Thanks, Pearson. You're definitely detective material," she said.

This time, Nelson did laugh but covered it by shifting to a cough. She shot him a glare and stepped past the young officer to the honeymooners.

"How are you guys doing?"

"I—I'm scared, Charlie. What is going on?" Monica clung to Will's side, tears streaking her cheeks.

"Yeah? This is insane. Is that— Is it Drake?" Will said.

"You know Drake Brown?" she said, not bothering to explain how she knew his full name. There was enough shock in the moment that they wouldn't question how she knew him.

They both nodded. "That's him," Monica said. "The guy I mentioned."

"Your ex-boyfriend," Charlie said. Will stiffened but didn't say anything, and Monica merely nodded. "And you were talking with him?"

"I wasn't really…" Monica looked up at Will. "We kind of had a fight tonight. It was stupid, I see that now."

"Were you working with clay?" Nelson asked from behind her. Charlie had picked up on traces of clay on Monica's hands too. She turned to glance at Nelson, but he gave nothing away in his expression.

"We were," Will admitted. "I felt bad that Monica's first pottery experience was bad, so I snuck us in to that private pool area and pulled up YouTube videos on my phone so we could learn how to do it together."

Charlie bit down her frustration. She'd offered to set them up with private lessons but hadn't heard back from them. Now was not the time for chastisement, though.

"It was fun," Monica said, her voice cracking. "But then Will had to take a call."

Will grimaced and looked toward the ocean. "I've just got a lot on my plate right now, and business can't be pushed aside—at least not completely."

"I got mad." Monica turned to face Will now. "I was wrong. Your work is important, and I know it's been weighing on you."

Charlie had caught that as well. The dark circles under his eyes, the weariness in his expression. She'd chalked it up to the loss of his USB and digital artwork—which would stress anyone out—but Monica seemed to think it was more about his current work.

"Yeah, but—"

"What is going on here?"

Charlie jumped despite herself and turned to face Detective Perez.

"Sophia—" Nelson began, but she turned toward him with a pointed finger.

"It's *Detective* Perez, and I want to know what in the world you thought you were doing by letting her speak to my suspect, Pearson?"

"W-what, ma'am?" Pearson stammered.

"And you." The detective rounded on Charlie. "What do you think you're doing?"

"She works at the hotel," Pearson said, finally finding his voice. "She wanted to console them."

"Looked more like an interrogation. Am I missing something?" Detective Perez turned to Charlie.

There was a moment when Charlie opened her mouth to reply with an honest answer, but the woman jumped ahead.

"Because I have a witness saying that you, Mrs.—" She checked her notepad. "Mrs. Chrisman, were arguing with the deceased on the beach not twenty minutes before he was found dead. How do you explain that?"

Charlie found herself turning to Monica as well, curious to hear her answer, but she looked back with wide, terrified eyes—mute.

"That's it. We want a lawyer," Will said.

The detective laughed. "Of course you do. We're taking you down to the station for questioning, and you," she said to Charlie, "can leave."

"Soph— Detective Perez," Nelson said, his tone turning gentle and persuasive, "we weren't stepping on toes here."

"Sure feels like it." She rounded on Pearson. "Let's go."

Charlie watched as the woman gripped Monica's arm and led her toward the unmarked car, Will following. Anger radiated off him, but he complied. At this point, that was the best option.

"What do you think's going on?" Nelson said from where he stood next to her, watching them leave.

"I don't know. But there's one thing I do know." Charlie felt his gaze on her. "I'm going to get to the bottom of this —no matter what Detective Perez says."

Nelson turned to her, but one of the younger security guards came up to her, breathing hard. "Ms. Davis?"

"It's Charlie, but what's up?"

He took a breath. "Mr. Simmons told me to come get you. Someone's ransacked the pottery class area."

9

THEY PUSHED THE GATE OPEN, and Charlie gasped. Pottery equipment was upended, clay was tossed about in chunks, and the pots that Nelson had brought as examples to show different techniques lay in shattered pieces on the ground.

"Oh, Nelson," Charlie reached for him, her fingers landed on the solid muscle of his arm. "I'm so sorry. I-I don't understand."

He clenched his jaw, but he didn't say anything. He merely walked across the pool deck to the overhang where the class had been set up. Crouching down, he picked up a piece of a beautifully crafted pot that had been glazed with blue-and-gold splatters.

"This was one of my favorites." He exhaled and stood. "But I can make it again."

"I'm sorry. I know it won't be the same."

"Maybe not…" He turned to look down at her. "But that's the beauty of pottery. Each piece comes out a little differently. Unique. It'll be just as beautiful in its own way." His gaze searched her features, and Charlie was suddenly aware of how close they stood.

"But what was the motive to do this?" she said, taking several steps back and toward the destruction.

"Will and Monica?" Nelson said.

"That doesn't seem right," she said. "Why admit they were doing pottery at all if they knew it was destroyed?"

"True. They had clay all over, though." He motioned to the wet clay in lumps on the ground. "And that would have accounted for this."

"I saw that." Then, something occurred to her. "The pots for the class!" She rushed to the back of the pool area and around the corner where Nelson had enlisted the help of the resort maintenance staff to set up a type of drying area in a big locker.

"Someone got into this cabinet," Nelson said. He pointed to the wet spots of clay, and Charlie's stomach clenched.

"Are they ruined too?" And with it, her chance to host another pottery class?

Nelson released a sigh. "They're here. I guess whoever had it out against my pottery and supplies didn't know about this. It looks like this pot is new." He pointed to one in the middle of the shelf. It was slightly misshapen but had good detail around the top ruffled edges.

"That must be the one Monica did," Charlie guessed.

"Must be. Well, that's at least *some* good news about this." He shifted to look at her. "I'm going to have someone help me take these to *Ceramica* tonight."

"Are you sure?" Her gaze took in the somewhat lopsided bowls and mugs.

"Positive. I've got plenty of room in the back and that way, we can feel confident they will be safe. I need to fire them soon anyway." He reached out and ran a hand around the lip of a mug. "They'll be safe there."

"I'll send an email to the guests to let them know of the change." Gratitude swelled in her chest. "Nelson saves the day again," she said with a chuckle.

"Hardly. This—" He turned around and looked at the mess. "—worries me, though."

"It doesn't fit, does it?" She shook her head and looked around. "First, Will's USB is stolen from his room. There are several men connected with Will at the hotel—one seeming to follow Monica—and then her ex-boyfriend shows up as well. Not only that, he's found dead. And then this? How does it connect?"

Nelson shook his head. "Maybe it doesn't?"

"What? You think this was done by someone who has a vendetta against pottery?"

His lips quirked. "Perhaps. Or they just don't like *my* pottery."

She chuckled despite the situation. That was one thing she liked about Nelson. No matter how bad things got, he always seemed to be able to ease the tension of a situation. His eyes held hers again, and she felt that same connection she had when they first came in. Something that, if she were honest with herself, scared her.

"Say, Charlie..." Nelson suddenly sounded unsure. "Would you, uh, want to have a drink with me tomorrow night? Maybe somewhere in town?"

She opened her mouth to say yes then hesitated. They had gone out for drinks several times since she'd arrived at the Pearl Sands, sometimes with Valentina and Stephen, other times just them, but at *La Cantina,* it was never *just* you and another person. There was always hearty conversation and laughs to fill the space between you.

But he was asking her to go *out* to get a drink. Was he asking her on a date in the middle of a ruin of pottery?

"You know, I don't know if I'll be able to," she said, shifting to step around him. She needed to connect with the security team to make sure someone was stationed here until they could get things cleaned up and the rest of the class's pottery safely to *Ceramica.* "You know how Felipe is. I've got a feeling I'll be looking into who could have done this." *As well as the murder on the beach.*

The mention of Felipe drew her thoughts back to his invitation for a drink as well. She'd turned him down, so it was only right that she turned Nelson down as well. She wasn't sure she was ready for what "getting drinks" meant —on any level and with anyone.

"Thanks, though. Another time, perhaps?" Charlie strove for a breezy tone. "I'm going to go speak with Ben and see if we can get some extra security here."

"Charlene." Nelson reached out and stopped her with a hand on her arm. The use of her full name sent shivers up her spine. "I'm not going anywhere."

She wanted to laugh and make a joke about him going home, but she saw his true meaning behind his hazel eyes shadowed by the accent lights. He was telling her it was alright to wait. That he would be there when she was ready. *If* she were ever ready.

"Have a good night, Nelson."

He nodded, and she turned away, heart pounding.

"HOW? HOW HAS THIS HAPPENED AGAIN?"

Charlie took on a mollifying attitude toward Felipe. "It's going to be all right. He wasn't found *on* the Pearl Sands beach."

"But it was Sands adjacent, and he was a guest," Felipe said, dropping his head into his hands. "*Dios mia,* what am I going to do?"

"Take a breath, to start with."

Felipe sat back and stared her down from his seat across from her. She'd met him in his office the next morning as he'd requested, but she'd found him in what she'd classify as "a state."

"I know it looks bad—"

"That's because it is." His laugh was just shy of actual humor. "The amount of bad press this will bring—"

"—is out of our hands. What is in our hands is finding the truth."

He seemed to calm at her words. "True. Have you made any progress on the USB?" His hopeful look sent a spike of self-frustration through her.

"Not yet. I need to check out Will and Monica's room. I need to see where it was taken from and ask Will a few more questions, but I don't even know if they're back." She'd explained how things had progressed the night before.

He nodded. "That is *one* good piece of news I can give you then. They arrived back around two in the morning. I was updated by Elijah."

Charlie nodded. "That is good news."

Felipe nodded. "Could you speak with them today?"

"Yes. If they'll let me. I also want to ask them about the pottery area too."

The expression of pain radiated across Felipe's tan Spanish features again. "I cannot believe that happened as well. Should I report the damage to Detective Perez?"

Charlie tamped down her first response, which was to cut out the angry detective trying too hard to prove herself. "If that's what you would normally do in a situation like this, then yes."

His eyes narrowed. "That was not as straightforward an answer as I have come to expect from you, Charlie. Is there something wrong?"

"Not wrong. I think the detective and I got off on the wrong foot is all." That was putting it mildly.

"She is a bit...driven, is she not?"

"How do you know her?"

Felipe shifted in his seat, dropping her gaze. "That is a long story, and I have many details to attend to today. Please, let me know if I can help you in any way."

She stood and met his gaze. "Thank you, Felipe. I know you want this to be wrapped up quickly, and I'll do my best."

"I believe that you will. *Gracias.*"

She dipped her head and left his well-appointed office. Charlie pulled out her phone and sent a text off to Monica and Will, hoping that she'd hear from them soon, and then she made her way to her desk.

The stack of black folders had grown overnight, and she set to work planning excursions and a few fishing trips now that the weather was better. The lobby filled with guests checking in and then emptied as they found their rooms, headed for the dining areas or pool, or leaving for day excursions.

It was just after lunch when Charlie got a text message back from Monica. She invited her to their villa at her convenience and promised they would answer her questions as best they could.

While Charlie had been glad to hear from them, she was also worried. Being back at her actual job reminded her of all the things she'd neglected over the last few days. There were emails, voicemails, and even a few written notes left by front desk personnel that she needed to respond to.

It brought her back to the night before and her offer of dinner to Juliana. In the chaos of that morning, she hadn't even had a chance to reach out to the young woman.

She shot off a quick text to Monica saying she'd be by within the hour and then got to work answering as many questions as she could. Then, before she left her desk, she sought out Juliana's email in the staff directory. The information was for anyone wanting to trade shifts or things of that nature, but Charlie offered her an apology for the disrupted night and the plans that had fallen through. She included her phone number and told Juliana to get in touch whenever she could.

Feeling somewhat more accomplish than she had before, Charlie set off for Villa Blanco. The most direct path took her through the pool area, and she scanned it for signs of Curt the gallery owner or Lucas the online gallery owner.

Strange that they'd both be at the resort where Will was honeymooning, but it was possible that was part of the business Monica had mentioned the night before. The things that seemed to cause Will stress.

She skirted around a group of grandmothers in matching t-shirts and stepped onto the path that led to each villa. She passed several and then knocked on the white door to Villa Blanco.

"Coming," a voice called from inside.

Monica opened the door and tried—and failed—to look happy to see Charlie. Her eyes were puffy, and she still had creases against her cheek as if she'd just woken up.

"I'm not disturbing you, am I?"

"No," Monica said, stepping back to allow her entrance. "I just fell asleep again after I texted you."

"I heard you both had a long night."

Monica sniffed as if she might burst into tears again, and Charlie heard Will call out, "Don't start that again, Mon. Really."

He came out of the door to the left that led to the primary suite. His air was wet, and he wore loose-fitting shorts and a tank top. "Hi, Charlie."

He seemed less affected than his wife, but Charlie knew Monica had been the main person of interest in Detective Perez's mind.

"That's easy for you to stay. You're not the one under investigation."

The words confirmed Charlie's suspicions. "Let's have a seat, shall we?"

Monica followed Charlie to the beige leather couch and sat while Charlie took a wingback chair opposite her. Will flopped down next to Monica, his arms stretching out across the back of the couch in a posture of relaxation.

"What happened last night?" she asked, directing the question to Will, who seemed able to handle the stress a little better than Monica.

"It was nuts," he admitted. "They took us down in that detective's car and treated us like we were suspects. Can you believe that?"

Charlie sensed he didn't mean it as a real question. "You asked for a lawyer," she prompted.

"Yeah. I've got some good connections, and the guy showed up fast. They questioned Mon, but there wasn't much to say."

"May I ask about the argument," Charlie said, shifting the conversation.

"With Drake?" She shot a look at Will, and Charlie wondered if he would care.

"Yes. Will this topic bother you, Mr. Chrisman?"

"Look, he's dead and that's tragic, but I've got no love lost for the guy."

Charlie's eyebrows rose. "I see."

"Not, like, in a way that I would want him to be dead, just that—what's in the past is past, you know?"

Charlie wasn't sure if she knew what he meant exactly, but she took it in stride. "Well, Monica?"

"I saw him on the beach when I was walking," she began. "I was kind of shocked to see him, actually. I mean, I knew he was at the resort, but I didn't think I'd actually run into him. It's a big place."

Charlie knew and nodded, looking for any signs of deception in the woman's story but seeing none so far.

"He tried to get me to talk to him—about why we broke up and stuff. I told him it was ancient history. That I was married now, and he needed to move on." She looked away now, reaching up to touch her nose. "Then I left."

"Are you sure you didn't say anything else to him?"

Monica bit her lip but didn't look up or reply.

"Mon?" Will said.

"I might have made a comment about how it looked like he'd already moved on." Heat flooded her cheeks. "I mean, it wasn't like I was jealous. It just rubbed me the wrong way. He took offense to the comment, and we started to argue. One of the reasons I left him for you." She looked over at Will, taking his hand. "It got heated, like it always does with him, so I left."

"And that was the last time you saw him?"

141

"Until...he was on the beach."

"Right." Charlie thought back to the night before. "Did you see anyone else on the beach?"

"No. That's why what the detective said was so strange. I know there was no one around. I looked."

She dropped her gaze again, but Charlie knew why this time. Monica hadn't wanted Will to see her and Drake talking. Which made sense but also made her sound guilty.

"Did the detective say anything else to you or ask you any other questions?" Charlie pressed, hoping to move past the awkward moment.

"Not really. I mean, she asked about Will's business and stuff. I think she was interested in the USB going missing, but there wasn't anything we could tell her, *and* she didn't tell us anything. I really think she's convinced I killed Drake, though."

"Which is insane," Will added. He shifted and kissed Monica on the cheek. "They'll find out how wrong they were as soon as they find out who really did it."

"And who do you think that is?" Charlie asked. She looked at both of them so they would know she was open to either of them answering.

"Who knows?" Will said.

"I mean, I haven't seen him in months before I saw him here," Monica said.

Charlie debated how much she wanted to press but decided to shift topics. "While I'm here, can you show me the hiding place where you had the USB?"

Will looked up from where he'd been staring at his phone. "What?"

"The USB that was stolen. I know the police are looking into it, but I'd still like to see where it was hidden."

"Uh, okay." He stood and beckoned her into the bedroom.

The sheets were mussed and the curtains drawn, so he threw them aside before pointing to his travel bag. It appeared just like any other bag, and she wondered if he'd hidden it in the lining or in a piece of clothing.

When he reached in an pulled out a book, she frowned. "A book?"

"Yep." He flipped it open and showed the hole that had been cut out of the pages on the inside. It was just the right size for a small USB.

"And was the book kept in your luggage?"

He tilted his head. "No, actually." He smiled now, as if realizing something. "You're smarter than you look."

She met his gaze head on. "I am a trained investigator. I may not be with the police, but I've solved my fair share of criminal cases." It wasn't exactly a defense of his comment, but she feared saying more and coming off sounding defensive.

"I had the book here." He moved past her and toward the far side of the bed. He pulled out the mattress a bit and pushed the book in front of the mattress. When he shoved the mattress back, it held the book in place but didn't look obvious. "I figured people might check under the mattress, but they wouldn't think much about a book stuck behind it."

"That was a risk, Mr. Chrisman. Can you tell me again why you decided to keep the USB with you instead of putting it in the hotel's safe?"

He shrugged. "I just like to be in charge of my own security."

It was on the tip of her tongue to point out how well that had gone for him, but she kept the words in. "I see. Well, thank you for showing me that."

They went back out into the main room, where Monica clutched a pillow to her chest with her chin resting on it.

"Mr. Chrisman, I think you're at the heart of all of this."

He looked over at her, surprise on every line of his features. "Me? How?"

"I think it started with you and your missing USB. It's now escalated to murder." She paused, drawing in a breath to make sure she said what she meant and that it came out right. "I think there are things you're keeping from the police—and from me—and I would very much like to know what those things are."

She held his gaze, all but arguing with him to open up to her, but it was a lost cause. She saw that the minute he broke into a smile.

"I'm not hiding anything, but if you happen to solve the murder and find my USB, that would be great."

"Will..." Monica's tone was admonishing.

"Hey, I get it, she's some bigwig P.I., but I'm going to wait out the police on this one."

Charlie blinked. It was completely opposite what he'd said when asking—nearly begging—her to look into this.

She nodded once and walked to the door, pausing to turn before she left. "One more thing..." She looked between them. "Did either of you see anyone go into the private pool area where the pottery class was held?"

They both wore blank expressions, but something in Monica's eyes drew her to narrow in on the woman. "Monica? Did you see someone?"

She sent a nervous glance to Will. "I thought, I mean I was probably wrong, but it looked like Curt was waiting outside when I left after you went to take that call."

"Curt Mulroney?" Charlie asked.

Will finally looked rattled when she said the man's name. "How do you know Curt?" he demanded.

"I'm a bigshot P.I., remember?" She smiled and slipped outside.

10

CHARLIE WAS FAIRLY certain she was being tailed. She'd left Monica and Will's villa and opted to take the beach back since she was scheduled for an afternoon break anyway and needed to sift through what she'd learned from the honeymooning couple.

Monica had seemed distraught, but was it too much? Was she acting? Or was she really as rattled as she acted? It was clear she and Drake hadn't had a good relationship, but was his murder about her or something else?

And Will. He'd appeared almost carefree—so much so that it contradicted how she'd expected him to act when they were talking about things like murder and his missing art. Was it possible he had a backup he hadn't mentioned, or was there more going on with his art than he was admitting?

She pulled out her phone and shot off a text to Valentina. If this *was* art-related, which made the most sense, she needed more information and perhaps Michael could get that for her.

Charlie paused in front of the ocean and turned to face it, her peripheral vision taking in the man thirty yards back. Yes, she was being followed but she didn't know who it was or why they'd be focused on her.

She didn't feel threatened, only warned. Was this about the murder or…

She turned then, fully looking the man in the eyes. He turned, pretending to be doing something else, but she'd caught his stare and his bearing.

Police.

Shrugging, she walked back to her desk. The police could trail her all they wanted—no doubt at Detective Perez's instruction—but they wouldn't find out anything important.

The chilled cucumber-water scented air of the lobby greeted her, and she jumped back into work with fervor. There were too many questions about Drake Brown and his murder. Too many things that didn't seem to match up.

How could Detective Perez really consider Monica as a suspect? She was short, about as tall as Charlie anyway, and it would have been quite the feat for a woman of her size to be able to kill a fit man like Drake.

She could admit that, from a quick preliminary look, the strangulation marks looked to have been made by rope, but still, for a woman to strangle a man to death... It would take a leap of logic to get to that point.

So, what was Perez's play?

Charlie leaned her chin on her fisted hand and stared at the shiny marble floor. The woman was smart, there was no doubt about that, and there was no way she could have missed the clay on Monica's hands—

Charlie sat up straighter. Clay. There hadn't been any clay on Will's hands. Was that it? Had Detective Perez accused his wife in order to get Will down to the station too? It seemed shoddy work. Why not come out and ask? There could be a reason she didn't understand, though.

She refocused on her computer and tapped on a few keys before a voice broke the silence. "Ms. Davis?"

"Yes?" She looked up, expecting to see a resort guest interested in her services, but her eyes locked with those of the officer who had been following her. "Officer," she added, so he would know she knew who he was.

"Officer Landry. Would you please come with me to the station? Detective Perez would like to question you about your involvement with events here at the Pearl Sands."

Charlie's eyebrows shot up. "The station? Really?" She almost wanted to ask if the detective could come to her workplace since they had to be on the scene investigating, but this felt more like a powerplay than anything else.

"Yes, ma'am. She's got some questions for you. She said it wouldn't take long."

"I don't have a car."

"I'm happy to drive you."

"Well then, Officer Landry, lead the way." She put up the sign on her desk saying that she would be away and followed the officer out into the bright sunlight. The valet brought his car around, and she made sure they comped the parking so that Landry wouldn't have to pay, even though the department would take care of it.

The drive to the station, which was much closer to the tied island than Charlie had realized, only took ten minutes. Soon, she was entering the air-conditioned space that felt at once foreign and familiar.

"This way," he said, gesturing for her to follow him.

They walked along a wall with desks to one side until he came to a small office, the door open.

"Detective Perez, she's here."

The detective looked up, her face a stone mask of indifference, and gestured Charlie inside.

"Ms. Davis, take a seat."

Charlie didn't like the commanding way she said it, but she wasn't here to make waves. At least she hadn't been taken to an interrogation room.

"How can I help you, Detective?"

"Help me?" The detective laughed. "More like, how can I help you stay out of my way."

Charlie blinked. "What is it you want?"

"I want to know how you noticed those ligature marks so quickly. I want to know why you were questioning my suspects. I want to know why you were even on the beach that late at night. And I want to know why you continue to be at the center of investigations."

The list the detective offered was a little surprising, but Charlie chalked it up to the fact that she was new in her role—that was obvious—and she was making a name for herself. It wasn't that Charlie thought she felt threatened, but she did feel the need to exert her dominance. Charlie could understand that in an abstract way.

"I noticed the marks because, as I said at the scene, I checked the man's vital signs and the red marks on his neck were hard to ignore. As I told you before, I'm a licensed private investigator trained in, well, investigation. I was speaking with Monica and Will because I have a rapport with them and wanted to see how they were holding up under the stress of such a situation." She paused, wondering if she wanted to share any of her suspicions with the woman.

"What were you even doing out there?"

Charlie took the next question in stride. "I was going to the south end to have dinner at *La Cantina* with a co-worker. We chose the beach way since it was a lovely night, and we happened to come across the small group of people who had gathered around Drake's body.

"As for your final question, my manager—the general manager of the Pearl Sands—asked me about helping out with the last investigation since Detective Neal was going to retire and he wasn't sure how much of the man's attention would be focused on the case. I was worried at first too, but it turned out that Don and I worked well together. It can be helpful to have someone on location when you're away." As she said the last part, she held the woman's gaze.

It wasn't so much that Charlie wanted to challenge her, but she was curious why the woman wasn't at the resort conducting interviews and investigating the murder. Perhaps she preferred to have everyone come to her, but it wasn't how Charlie would do things.

"I see." Detective Perez held Charlie's gaze for a moment before breaking it to look at her notes. "I don't like you being involved in this."

Charlie opened her mouth to respond then closed it. It was clear that there were other things going on here, things she didn't fully understand about the woman or her role in this new position, so she waited.

Finally, Perez looked up again. "Officer Landry informed me you went to talk to Mr. and Mrs. Chrisman again today. What was that conversation about?"

"Why do you need to know what a hotel staff person would say to two guests?" Charlie felt bad the minute she'd said it, it was petty, but she waited to see how the detective would respond.

"Don't play games with me, Ms. Davis. Why did you talk to them? Monica is a person of interest in the case of Drake Brown's murder, and you are clearly investigating something. I need to know what."

"Answer me one question first," she challenged. Perez remained silent so Charlie took that as permission. "How can you honestly think Monica, standing at, what—five feet two inches, maybe—could be responsible for killing a tall, muscular man like Drake?"

Detective Perez narrowed her eyes and leaned forward on her desk. "You'd be surprised what a woman can do when an adult male is heavily intoxicated."

Charlie did her best not to let the information show on her face, but she must have missed the mark because the detective leaned back and inhaled sharply. "I shouldn't have said that."

"I still don't believe it." Charlie gave the woman a distraction to focus on.

"Don't believe—" Detective Perez shook her head. "If you think by some misguided idea that you're going to waltz in here and solve my case, you are sorely mistaken. I've known women like you. Doing all they can to maneuver their way past regulations and do the 'fun' thing of investigative work. And you know what happens?"

The silence hung between them, so Charlie answered what she'd assumed was a rhetorical question. "What?"

"They get hurt." Sophia flinched. The movement was so slight that Charlie almost missed it, but then the woman looked to the side, and Charlie felt like she was reading the woman's life story. And there was definitely a story there.

"Detective Perez," she said in her most calming voice. "I'm sorry that you think I'm intruding on your case. Felipe Delgado asked me to look into the theft of Will's USB drive since it occurred on Pearl Sands property. That's what I've been doing. Finding Drake's body—though I was not the first on the scene—was purely coincidence." She held up a hand. "And before you say what I think you will, I don't believe in coincidences either, but in this case, I see no other way around it." Charlie picked up her purse and stood, the sensation of buzzing coming from the side pocket where her phone was.

"What are you doing?"

"We both know you aren't going to hold me here—there are no charges that will stick for that—and I think you've gotten all you wanted from me." *I certainly have from you.* "Good day, Detective."

Charlie spun and walked out of the room, wondering if the slight woman might jump over her desk to come after her. It was something she looked more than capable of doing.

But as Charlie neared the front desk and pushed out of the security door to the main lobby, there was no sound of pursuit behind her.

The warm sun on her face seeped past the chill that had overtaken her in the police station—both from the air conditioning and the detective. It was clear the woman had experienced something painful in the past, but what Charlie couldn't figure out was how that translated to this case—and to her.

She pulled out her phone, remembering the vibrating she'd felt in the office, and noticed that Valentina had called her several times and left a few text messages. She quickly flipped to the messaging app.

VALENTINA: Michael has news.

VALENTINA: About the guy who died, that is. Can you go see him?

SEVERAL MINUTES LATER, she'd sent:

VALENTINA: Stephen and I can meet you there when you're done. Elijah said you left with an officer? Sending the address. Call me when you're free.

CHARLIE CHECKED THE ADDRESS—LIKELY the gallery that Michael managed—and texted Valentina her ETA. She paused, her finger hovering over the app that would call up the Uber to take her to the gallery.

If there really was news about Drake Brown, she should bring the detective. The thought soured in her stomach.

The woman was blinded by her own aspirations and whatever she felt she had to prove.

No. Charlie physically shook her head as if to solidify her choice to keep the detective out of the loop—at least for the moment. She'd tell the woman when the time was right.

THE UBER PULLED up in front of a two-story gallery with a large sign that merely said *Pinnacle* in two-foot-high letters made of chrome. The style of the building was ultra-modern with clean lines and cream-and-steel accents.

Entering through the double-doors, the scent of oil paint and something reminiscent of vanilla greeted her. Calming music played over hidden speakers and accent lighting set a muted tone throughout the gallery.

She turned to look at the front windows and realized that, while you could see in well from outside, the light dimmed as it came inside. That had to be a preservation technique for the art.

Walking down the main aisle, she passed metal sculptures, pottery, and even a few modern pieces of art made from everyday household items. Charlie didn't understand it, at least not in the way of classical art, but she wasn't an artist.

"Ah, Ms. Davis?"

Charlie looked up from where she'd been studying a beautiful, hyper-realistic marble sculpture. "Are you Michael?"

"I am. It's nice to meet you." He held out his hand and she shook, turning her attention to the art on the walls around them. "These are incredible. And please, call me Charlie."

Michael grinned. "You got it. I've heard nothing but good things from Valentina."

"Oh?"

"My sister and I are very close. She works a lot and it's hard to get over to see her and Stephen when I work on this side of town, but we try to do dinner every week if we can."

"I'm glad to finally meet you in person. I too have heard good things." She walked around him to another piece. It looked familiar. "Have you always been into art?"

"Ever since I was a kid. I dabble in oils and some clay sculpture, but I found my true calling was more about managing." He offered a congenial laugh, and Charlie smiled. "Val says they are almost here. I… I've got a friend who wants to speak with you."

Charlie pulled her gaze from the walls. "They are here now?"

"In the back." He shifted from one foot to the other. "I kind of had to convince him to talk. He's a little jumpy right now."

"How so?"

"I think he's afraid that what he knows will get him into some type of trouble."

Charlie's pulse ticked up. "Has he told anyone else? Besides you?"

"Not that I know of."

"How did he know to come to you?" She'd only spoken on the phone once with Michael.

"He didn't. Not really. We grabbed brunch today and got talking about Drake Brown's death. He mentioned to me that he knew him, and I started to dig a little." Michael looked sheepish.

"Good for you," Charlie said with a grin. "He opened up to you?"

"He did, and that's when I knew I needed to call you."

"I'm glad you did. I—" A soft chime cut into their conversation, and she turned to see Valentina and Stephen come in.

"Sorry we're a few minutes later than we thought. Stephen took a wrong turn."

"That you told me to take," Stephen added, not quite under his breath.

Valentina looked at him, and he made a gesture as if to say, *What's a guy supposed to do?*

Charlie laughed, and Michael stepped in, meeting his sister's gaze. "Yen's in the back."

"Is he freaking out?" Valentina asked.

"Totally."

Charlie watched the exchange between brother and sister. "You know his friend?"

"Yes. He's a sweet guy, but a little too into conspiracy theories, if you ask me."

"He's not that bad," Stephen added, sending a glance at his wife. "He just believes there are aliens and the government is keeping it from us."

"Oh yes, totally reasonable," Valentina added with an eye-roll.

"Let's go have a chat with him, if he's willing?" Charlie said, deciding to curtail any further discussion.

"Sure. This way."

She followed Michael's tall form through the rest of the gallery. He wore a dark suit and leather shoes that made no sound on the shiny concrete floor. They turned a corner, and a row of offices filled one side of the back area. They were closed off by floor-to-ceiling glass—as if the windows were on the inside rather than outside.

"We're very transparent here at Pinnacle," Michael said, by way of explanation.

"I see that." She also saw the young man she assumed they were going to talk to. Yen, if she'd heard that correctly.

He sat in a chair in the last office. He wore overly baggy jeans, a white button-up shirt, and a massive red-and-blue leather jacket. His dyed-blond hair showed dark roots, and he had several face and ear piercings.

More than his attire, Charlie took in his posture. His shoulders were slumped, and he continued to bounce his knee up and down. His hands were also an indication of his state of mind. They gripped one another enough to show white on his knuckles.

Michael opened the door, and the young man looked up. "Hey, Yen, this is Charlie Davis."

"Hi," he greeted her with a hooded look.

"Have a seat," Michael said, gesturing to another chair facing the young man. He slipped behind what she assumed was his desk, while Valentina and Stephen shuffled toward the couch with its back to the glass wall.

"Hi, Yen," Valentina said with a warm smile. "We need to have you over for pozole again."

"Yeah. That would, uh, be great." His knee bounced more furiously, and his eyes jumped from Val to Charlie to Michael and back to the floor.

"Listen, Yen, Michael told me that you have some information about Drake Brown." Charlie spoke softly so as not to startle the boy, but the mention of Drake's name caused him to react like he'd been shocked by an outlet.

"I—I don't know. Maybe I shouldn't say anything." His tongue shot out, licking his dry bottom lip.

"I get it. It's a scary thing to know something about someone who's died—"

"He was murdered!" Yen blurted.

"True." Charlie infused her voice with calm. "But, knowing the case as I do, I don't think you're going to be in any danger."

"How do you know?"

"I'm not positive," she admitted, "but I think that whatever is going on is isolated to the Pearl Sands—at least for now."

His eyes shifted away, and his knee bounced again. "I don't know."

"Just tell her, man," Michael said.

Yen shot his friend a look and then met Charlie's gaze. "I was at a party with Drake a few months ago, and I overheard him bragging about leverage."

Charlie did her best not to react to the fact that he was finally talking. She didn't want to spook him by being overeager, but this already sounded promising. "What kind of leverage?"

"I was a little, you know, tipsy at the time, but I got closer because I'm nosy." He shot Michael a look, his posture relaxing as he grew comfortable. "He started talking about

Will Chrisman. I know of Will, but I don't know him. He's like a phenomenon, you know?"

"So I've heard," she said.

"Drake was telling this lady that he had something on him. That he was going to drain him dry—whatever that means."

"Did he say what it was?"

"Yeah." Yen looked at Michael again. "And…I don't know —I mean, I can't prove this or anything—but he said that Will was using AI-generated art and passing it off as his own."

Charlie frowned. "You lost me, Yen."

"What he means," Michael interrupted, "is that Will was utilizing art created by an AI—artificial intelligence—in his digital work."

"And that's not allowed?" She guessed.

"No. Well…" Michael tipped his head from side to side. "It depends. Will has been bold about saying that his 'new art' is coming from a 'deep place' and things of that nature, but if what Drake said was true and he was utilizing AI-created art in his pieces, it could ruin his credibility."

"Is it just not allowed?" Valentina asked from her spot on the couch.

"It's not so much that it's not allowed but more that it's disingenuous."

"If he was going fully digital," Yen cut in on Michael, "then yeah, that'd be a big no-no. He'd lose all credibility."

"Would it jeopardize his chances with a place like ArtistOcean?"

"Oh yeah." Yen's head nodded so violently that his hair fell into his eyes. "They are, like, premium and would not stand to have an artist not have original art on there. It's a big deal."

"I see." Charlie nodded, placing new pieces together.

"Was that all you overhead, Yen?"

"Pretty much. I just remembered that convo this morning because Drake was so confident. I mean, he's—he *was*—just a model, but he acted like he knew art better than some of the best artists in Florida. It was a shock to hear he'd died, but maybe not. You know?"

Charlie nodded and stood. "Thanks for sharing that with us, Yen, but you're not going to like what I have to say next."

The young man's eyes widened. "What?"

"You need to go tell the police."

"Nah. No way." He shook his head. "That's how people end up dead. They talk to the cops."

She tried and failed to hide a placating smile. "In the movies, maybe, but no one will know that it was you who gave the tip. Talk to Detective Sophia Perez. She's in charge of the case and she'll help you." Charlie hoped that statement was true.

"I'll go with you," Michael offered.

"Thanks," Yen said. His shoulders slumped, and Charlie knew she'd convinced him.

"We'll give you a ride back, Charlie," Stephen said as he stood and offered a hand to his wife to help her up.

She followed them out and climbed into the back of Stephen's sedan. He started the car and pulled into the afternoon traffic. Valentina turned around in her seat to face Charlie.

"Work this out for me, Charlie. Who could have killed Drake?"

Charlie took in a deep breath. "This information is helpful, but I don't know that it narrowed down the suspects much. Well, it might have a little."

"How so?" Stephen asked, meeting her gaze for a second in the rear-view mirror.

"If Drake had the evidence he claimed to, then that puts him at odds with several people. First of all, Will." She swallowed, wondering if the man whose room she had just been in earlier that day could be a coldblooded killer. "Monica would also have motive, seeing as she seems to truly love her husband and wants the best for him."

"But to commit murder." Valentina shook her head. "That's a big leap."

"True," Charlie agreed. "Then there's Lucas Vello. Assuming Will was as big of a deal as it seems he is, then he wouldn't want the information about Will's digital art getting out either. The only person who doesn't factor into this is Curt Mulroney, and yet he's been at the Pearl Sands this whole time."

"Who did it then?" Valentina asked.

Charlie sensed she wasn't really asking her for the answer, but it was a good question. "The only way for us to know is to dig deeper. To see where everyone was and to figure out which motive was strong enough to cause someone to act with violence."

It sounded easy, laid out like that, but Charlie knew from experience that it wouldn't be. She'd need help.

"Valentina, are you willing to help me on this?"

"Of course. Anything you need."

"What about me?" Stephen asked.

"I think I've got something you could help me with too." Charlie allowed a small smile as her plan began to take shape in her mind.

They were going to get to the bottom of Drake's murder and the theft of Will's USB.

11

CHARLIE SAW Monica before the woman noticed her and took a moment to observe. Was she the type who would have gone to great lengths to protect her husband? Could she have killed her ex-boyfriend? From their past conversations, it sounded as if she and Drake hadn't gotten along well while they were dating, but that didn't automatically translate to murder.

Plenty of people broke up with boyfriends and didn't turn around and kill them.

Still, as Charlie watched her, she thought she saw the shadow of burden cross Monica's beautiful features. She wore sunglasses, but she kept looking around like someone might be watching her. Someone was, but Charlie wasn't ready to step from her hiding place just yet.

Her phone buzzed in her pocket, and she pulled it out. It was a text from Valentina confirming what Charlie already knew. On the day Will and Monica checked into the hotel, Drake Brown and Curt Mulroney had also checked in. She knew from personal experience that Lucas had checked in a few days later. The USB had already been taken by then, but that didn't rule him out. If he was local, it was possible he'd come and taken it and then checked in after the fact. It felt farfetched and Charlie didn't really believe it, but it was a possibility.

The next phase of their plan was initiated by another text from Valentina saying that Stephen had gotten the meeting. It was a small lie, one she felt bad for asking Stephen to spin, but he'd agreed quickly.

He would pose as an art reporter for a well-known online magazine that wanted to feature the new rumored deal between Lucas Vello and Will Chrisman. He was using the cover that it had been leaked to him by one of Will's PR people, and she only hoped that Lucas didn't check up on that before meeting with Stephen.

They'd decided on the questions he'd ask, and he was prepping for the role as she stood watching Monica, the next person on Charlie's list.

Charlie texted back to Valentina reminding her to check the logs. She responded with a winking emoji, and Charlie wondered if she was being overbearing. It was odd, having friends to help her like this, but she liked the sense of teamwork.

The next step was getting a list of entry and exit timestamps from the computer system, which would help them know when people had been in, or out, of their rooms.

She was about to step from the shelter of her hiding spot when she caught sight of Ben across the pool area. She'd gone to his office to talk with him, but he'd been out, and the officer in the booth hadn't known when he'd be back.

What was the higher priority—getting a look at the security footage or speaking with Monica? When she looked back toward the woman, Charlie ground her teeth. Will had joined his wife, which meant Charlie's plan wouldn't work. Charlie had been sure when he left to take the call he would be gone for enough time to allow her to put a few hard questions to Monica, but that chance was gone.

It seemed fate—or something deeper than that—had chosen for her.

Spinning around, she followed Ben from a distance as he walked toward the main security office. There were three locations spanning the massive resort—something Charlie understood. Security in a place like this was a big job, and she was certain there had been video of Villa Blanco when the USB was stolen, but Detective Perez hadn't said a word about the theft. Will and Monica hadn't mentioned it either after their night at the station.

Either the detective was withholding the information, something Charlie wouldn't put past her, or the video had been a bust. She wouldn't know until she saw it with her own eyes.

Ben paused at the card reader outside the exterior office door, and Charlie made her approach.

"Saw you following me, Ms. Davis," he said without looking up.

She was impressed, though she hadn't tried for stealth. "I'd like a word with you if you have some time? I've also got a favor to ask."

His eyebrows rose, but he didn't say anything. Instead, he dipped his head toward the door and ushered her inside.

The space was chilly, much cooler than the rest of the resort. "The monitors put out a lot of heat so we need to keep it cold in here," he explained, as if reading her mind. It was likely a question he got a lot of when anyone came into the office.

"Makes sense," she said. Her gaze traveled dover the bank of monitors on the walls to the right and left. A man sat facing each bank of video screens, neither looking up or even acknowledging them. She assumed they had seen them coming but also knew that no one had access without a keycard.

"Follow me." He turned to the right and led her down a short hallway. They passed a one-stall bathroom, a small breakroom with an apartment-sized refrigerator, microwave, and circular table before he stopped at another door, pulling a key from an extendible keyring on his belt.

"Welcome to my office," he said, sliding into a chair behind the desk.

"Thanks," she said, taking a seat opposite him. "I just have a few questions."

"I bet you have more than a few." His narrow-eyed look landed on her with force.

"Not sure what that means, but perhaps I do."

"I can't quite figure you out, Ms. Davis."

"It's Charlie, remember?" She'd told him multiple times to call her by her first name, but he insisted on remaining formal. Well, if he were going to play hardball, she'd get in the game herself. "Look, *Mr.* Simmons, I get that you don't like me, but I am no threat to you or your job. I'm just doing what Felipe has asked and looking into a few things. Besides, I have all the credentials if you'd like me to recite them."

He steepled his fingers and stared back at her for so long she thought he might hold out until she spoke again, but she waited him out.

"Ms.— Charlie," he finally said, a sigh escaping as he used her first name. "I don't dislike you. I hardly know you, and I like to reserve those types of judgment for after a time when I've gotten to know someone. I do, however, dislike the position Felipe has put you in without first consulting me and without considering what it all means for the Pearl Sands."

"What do you mean?"

"Having a free agent that is not part of my security team—"

"You mean under your control?" She didn't blink.

"I suppose you could say that," he finally admitted. "It's dangerous. We do things as a team and that is how success is accomplished. As for the Pearl Sands, I think it opens us up to some difficult situations. A left-hand right-hand situation."

"You mean that, without communication, we're likely to move into the realm of questionable decisions?" She felt as if she understood what he was hinting at. If the right hand didn't know what the left hand was doing, it could create issues all round, but he wasn't giving her any credit. Then again, why should he.

"Something like that."

"I respect what you do here, Ben. I do. But I also know that your men are trained in resort security. They aren't trained investigators. Half of them aren't even out of college." She gave him a knowing look, but he offered no denial. "I *am* trained, and I am working within the confines of the rules I've been given. Short of reporting to you for duty, something I'm not likely to do, I don't see how else we can get past this unless we start to trust one another."

"I read your file," he said when she'd finished. "I know a little of what happened in your past and...frankly, that worries me."

Charlie swallowed. The mention of her past tended to have the effect of closing her off, but she fought that in the moment. "When you say past, do you mean over twenty years ago? Because I assume you have met people who have changed from who they were when they were younger."

His eyebrow twitched. "You have a point."

"I'm not trying to take over your job. I'm not trying to work against you and your team either. I *am* trying to get to the bottom of things, and if you're not going to help me do that, then I should probably spend my time elsewhere."

She stood and hated the fact that her knees shook. It wasn't that she wanted to be at odds with Ben, it was just the opposite, but she wasn't sure what she could do to change his mind.

"Wait," he called out just before she pulled the door open. "What do you need?"

"A look at the cameras outside of Villa Blanco during the night that the USB went missing."

"The police already looked at the footage. There's nothing there."

"Then there's no harm in seeing myself."

He pressed his lips together and, after an eternity, nodded. "Fine. Here." His fingers flew across the keyboard then he stood, pushing his chair back. "Have a seat."

She did, and he tapped the spacebar to start the video.

"This is a few minutes before Mr. Chrisman said he and his wife left their villa to go to dinner. They specifically told one of my security guys that they left out the back to take the beach since it was a nice night."

Charlie nodded and watched when the couple came out of the gate. Will had his arm around Monica, and they were laughing. He pulled her close and kissed her temple then she stopped him with a hand on his chest.

"What's she doing?"

"You'll see." Ben folded his arms over his chest and nodded toward the screen.

Monica rushed back through the gate and came back out a few minutes later with a pashmina wrap.

"She forgot something." Charlie said the words out loud, but they were to herself as a thought began to form in her mind.

"Pretty standard. No one comes in through the back gate or the front. At least not this villa."

She turned toward him. "Say that again."

"What? We didn't see anyone else come in or out of the front or back gates of Villa Blanco."

"No, the last part."

"Of this villa?"

"Exactly." Charlie stood and rushed around the desk. "Could you do me a favor? Check through the security

172

footage for Villa Amarillo and Villa Roja and send me any clips from around this time? I've got an idea, but I need to see those clips first."

"I—" He hesitated.

She stopped at the door. "I know, Ben. You don't trust me, but if anything, trust this—I've gotten countless criminals arrested. I've built air-tight cases and made a lot of clients happy with what I've uncovered. I'll sit down over coffee and explain my past to you if that's what it takes, but right now, we're running out of time."

"Fine. I'll do it."

She held his gaze for a moment longer then, with a nod, she left the security office and headed toward the front desk. She had alibis to check.

"Did you look up what I asked?" Charlie slipped into Valentina's office and closed the door behind her.

"Yes, but I'm worried I could get in trouble for accessing this information." Valentina looked up nervously at Charlie.

"I will stand up for you to Felipe if there's an issue. He's given me access to do what I need to in order to work this case."

"But what about the police?"

Charlie scrunched up her nose. "I'm not sure. I don't know that it's against the law to access room exit and entry logs. You could make a case that it helps you with your job."

Valentia barked a mirthless laugh. "I don't think that will fly. But, oh well. Let's go."

Her fingers flew across the keys, and Charlie took up a position behind her. "Right there," Charlie said, pointing.

"I see it." Valentina clicked on the name. "You were right. He's in Villa Roja. Has been since the day the USB drive went missing."

"And the other side?"

"Amarillo? Vacant until Lucas Vello checked in. Just like you thought."

Charlie stood up. "Check the access logs now."

With a few more clicks of the keys, Valentina opened the card reader logs. "At the time you sent me, it looks like Curt was in his villa." She searched back with a finger almost touching the screen. "He entered at around four that afternoon and didn't leave until the next morning."

"Does that register the back gates to the beach as well?"

Valentina nodded. "As far as I know, yes."

"But it doesn't negate my idea."

"You mean that he climbed over the wall into their garden area while they were gone?"

"Yes."

"But wouldn't the police have found evidence of that?"

"Not if Monica forgot to lock the door." Charlie said the words more to herself than Valentina, but something else struck her. "What if she didn't forget?"

Valentina met her gaze. "What do you mean?"

"It's possible she left the door unlocked but did so on purpose."

"Why? So someone could come in and take the USB drive? Do you think she had time to tell them where it was? I mean, from what you said, it sounded like a complicated hiding place."

"Not if she already knew about it. Wouldn't a husband tell his new wife where his most-valuable information was?"

"I suppose it depends on how much he trusted her."

"Good point." Charlie looked back at the screen. "Okay, one last look. Where was Drake during this time?"

Valentina's pink nails clicked on the keyboard until she pulled up his info. "In his room, actually."

Charlie bit her lip. "Could he have gone out a window?"

"He was on the third floor."

"Rats." Charlie stepped from behind her friend's desk and began to pace.

"Are you trying to pin something on a dead man?"

Charlie's gaze snapped to Valentina's. "Absolutely not. I just had a theory, and that's shot if he really was in his room."

"It looks that way."

"I still think my theory about Curt maybe right. While he's not a young man, he could certainly pull up a lawn chair and make it over the top of the stucco wall to drop down into their courtyard. Monica leaves the door open, he goes to where she told him the USB would be, messes up the room to make it less obvious he knew where to look, and gets out of there before they are even into their dessert course."

"Evidence. I think you need some of that."

Charlie smirked at Valentina. "I know. It's all speculation, but it's something to go off of."

"What will you do next?"

"I think I need to speak with Curt."

"Are you crazy?" Valentina came out from behind her desk as well and faced Charlie with a shocked expression.

"No, but there's no better way to know what he's really thinking—or lying about—than meeting him face-to-face."

"But what if he's a killer?"

"The truth must out, Val. Besides..." She tilted her head. "I think I'll bring Nelson along."

"For security, scare tactics, or moral support?'

"All three." She kissed Valentina's check and went to the door. "Thanks for your help."

"Don't thank me yet. This info has to help you first."

"It will." Charlie let herself out of her friend's office with renewed determination. Things were finally starting to come together.

12

CHARLIE TOOK quick steps down the path toward Luxury Square. She needed to see if Nelson was in *Ceramica.* He hadn't answered his phone, which was very unlike him, and she didn't know any other way to get in touch with him.

She would have considered going to his house on the south end of the island, but she realized she didn't know where it was. His shop would be her first—and easiest—stop, and if he was there, she'd go to *La Cantina.*

"*Señorita* Charlie?"

"Jorge? Hello. Are you headed to the lobby? Did I mess up on a reservation?"

"No, not at all, *Señorita.* I had a break and was visiting with my sister on her lunchbreak but wanted to see if you had heard the news."

"News? What news?"

"About *Señor* Nelson's shop."

"No. I haven't heard anything." A fist of fear clenched her stomach. "What happened?"

"His shop was broken into. A mess everywhere. All his beautiful pottery—destroyed."

Charlie gasped. She couldn't comprehend what the man was saying. "His— *Ceramica*? It's destroyed?"

"*Si*. Very bad.'"

Numbness made Charlie's legs stiff, but she nodded and stumbled around the corner to the path that led to the upscale shopping area. Things like what Jorge said didn't happen in areas like this. There were cameras everywhere, and people knew better than to do something in broad daylight.

When she burst into the open from the path from the resort to the shops, she caught sight of several uniformed officers in front of *Ceramica*. Nelson was there as well, his sandaled feet exchanged for heavy work boots—no doubt due to the glass.

It was like he'd sensed her coming. His gaze shifted and he locked eyes with her. While she was still just getting to know the man, she could tell—even from a distance—that he was in pain. Her response surprised her as a mutual ache blossomed in her chest. It wasn't that she was surprised to care for her new friend's pain, but the depth of it caught her off guard.

Charlie quickened her steps, and the scene became clearer. Glass from the large front window lay shattered on the sidewalk. The police had erected a tape line that she assumed was to keep pedestrians safe as they talked with Nelson.

The gaping hole in the window was not the only broken glass. The door was also shattered and revealed more destruction inside.

"Oh, Nelson." The words came out on a breath.

"It's worse inside," he said with what she assumed was forced levity.

"We're done for now, Mr. Hall. We'll get in touch with you when we have any news to share. For now, my guys will finish up here as fast as they can."

"Thanks so much," he said, nodding to the police officer, who flipped his notebook closed and turned toward the other officers processing the scene. "There's no rush."

"What happened?" Charlie asked, though she knew the question was a foolish one. It was clear, at least on the outside, what had happened.

"Some kid with a vendetta against pottery went to town on the shop." Nelson roughed a hand over his jaw. "I never would have expected this here."

"Did the cameras pick up anything? They must have recorded something?"

He shrugged. "I checked. It was the first thing we looked at. All that's shown is a man—boy?—wearing a black hoodie, gloves, and black face-covering bust in the front window and go on a smashing rampage."

"No identifying features? I assume your video is good."

"It is. It looks like it could be a teen, but it was hard to know for sure with the face being covered. He had a lean build, though."

"I'm so sorry, Nelson," she said again.

"Let's take a look inside. They said they've dusted the main areas for prints, but we could clearly see him wearing gloves, so it was useless. Anything they find will just be past customers, I'm sure. Although there was one area where it looks like the guy cut his hand."

"Did they get blood?"

Nelson couldn't help but smile a little. "He picked up all the bloody pieces, but he missed this." He pointed to a spot on the floor where an expensive rug had a square hole cut out of it.

"A drop?"

"Yep.

"Well, that's something."

He nodded, and she followed him inside the shop. Her audible gasp echoed against the smooth walls, but she couldn't keep it in. Everything was shattered.

"Did he have a brick with him? A bat? This level of damage seems like overkill."

"I agree. We saw him with something like a crowbar in his hand. That's what I guess he used."

"I'm sure the police already asked you this, but—"

"No, I don't have any enemies." Nelson eyed her. "I've been on both ends of the investigation, Charlie. You know that."

"I had to ask."

"I know. And honestly, I can't think of anyone. Especially not anything that would be triggered at this time."

The way he said it made her wonder if there were other times when he would expect something like this, but she bypassed that knowing he would have shared if it were pertinent.

"The only thing I can think of is the pottery class."

His words snapped her thoughts from their analyzing. "What?"

"I told the police this, but the class was demolished and then I brought the salvaged pots here to be fired. That's the only connection I have to violence."

"Are those pots destroyed then?"

"Most had already been fired, but—" He paused. "Wait a second."

Nelson turned and headed toward the backroom. Charlie followed. It was also wrecked, yet the computer hadn't been touched. To Charlie, that was a small mercy, but she'd take it. The shelves held shattered pots of all shapes and sizes, and she was again reminded of how much damage this person had done. It would take Nelson months to remake even half of his inventory—or so she assumed. She didn't actually know much about how he ran his business.

"I didn't even think to check these when the police arrived. "He stepped toward the back of the room and out a side door into a small courtyard where a kiln sat. "I was going to fire these today but hadn't gotten around to it."

When he opened the door, Charlie smiled down at a layer of pots ready to be fired.

"Are those all from the class?"

"Some are mine, some are from the class. Monica's pot is here, actually." He reached down and picked it up. "I thought it was going to be rather nice."

She extended a hand, and he placed the small vase in it. She admired the shape and smooth lines. It was clear Monica was artistic. "I think I can see how it would be really beautiful once it's done." She shifted it around, but something scratched against her palm in the process. "What's this?"

Nelson took the ceramic vase and turned it over. His forehead furrowed as he ran a thumb over a bulge in the bottom. "It looks like something's *in* the clay. Follow me."

DANIELLE COLLINS & MILLIE BRIGGS

He took a moment to close the kiln and then headed inside with the vase in hand. He looked at a bench were tools sat and plucked one up. Before she could stop him, he began scraping away at the object.

"Be careful," she warned.

He sent her an amused look. "I will. Remember, clay is what I do."

She blushed. "Of course."

He worked quickly and expertly, Charlie could tell that much, and soon he made one last swipe then held out the vase to show her.

"Is that—"

He nodded. "A USB drive? Yes."

"In Monica's vase."

"Yes."

Charlie met Nelson's gaze. "We need to talk to Curt Mulroney."

"Want to tell me why we're seeing Curt, not Monica?"

"Oh, we'll see Monica too, but first I need to confirm a suspicion I have." Charlie opened a side door into the resort and Nelson walked in, the bag with the vase held carefully in both hands.

184

"Which is?" He sent a gaze her way, but her eyes were focused ahead.

"It's a hunch, but I don't think it's unreasonable."

"Why don't you fill me in first and then make excuses?" He chuckled.

Charlie rolled her eyes. "Aside from Will, I think that Curt has the most to lose if Will goes digital with his art. Will is a big name and this decision would affect the Rockford Gallery significantly—or so I guess." She paused at the door that would lead them out into the main resort area. "I think that Monica could be working with Curt. The video showed her going back into their villa the night the USB was stolen. I think she purposefully left the slider open and Curt, who was in Villa Roja next door, slipped over the wall, got the USB, and disappeared."

"Then how did it end up in Monica's pot?"

Charlie opened her mouth then closed it. "I'm not sure."

"Sounds like you're guessing, Ms. Davis."

"Not exactly. But that's also why I want to talk to Curt first. I want to confirm—or amend—my suspicions before I talk to Monica."

"And you think he's just going to, what, tell you the truth?" Nelson looked incredulous.

"With the right pressure, maybe." She grinned and pushed the door open. "Curt's villa is on the other side of the resort. I think if we cut through the pool area, it'll be fastest."

"Shouldn't we call the police about the USB?"

"Yes, but I think it's just the leverage we need first."

Nelson stopped her with a gentle hand on her arm. "Charlie, you're playing a dangerous game. Detective Perez won't like being kept out of the loop like this."

Charlie's eyes narrowed. "How exactly do you know the detective?"

"That's a story for another time," he said with a tightlipped smile. "I just want to make sure I've covered my bases and warned you."

"Consider me warned. Now come on."

They stepped into the main pool area and were met with a crowd of sunbathing bodies. The weather had shifted to a very warm day, and everyone was enjoying time in the sun or splashing through the water.

Charlie was about to suggest they take the service hallway when a barked word from behind them stopped them in their tracks.

"Nelson."

They both turned and saw Detective Sophia Perez walking toward them, two officers trailing her.

"Charlene Davis." The detective met Charlie's stare with an icy one of her own. "I just got a call from the head of security that you've got information on the case. Funny, I don't recall you reaching out to me about it. Follow me."

The woman's tone left no room for argument, so Charlie and Nelson fell in line behind her.

They entered the overly cool security office, and Charlie did her best not to glare at Ben Simmons. He hadn't given her the courtesy of asking if she'd reached out to the police, he'd assumed she hadn't. Rightly so, but still.

Charlie knew this was her only chance to convince the woman that she was not out to take her job but also to make sure she knew that there were several clues that needed looking at.

"Why don't you tell me, Ms. Davis, why you think that you can go around doing whatever you want on these hotel grounds? And why you think it's okay to interfere with police business?"

Charlie cut a look at Ben, she couldn't help it, but he wouldn't meet her gaze. "I don't think that's okay, but I do have information I'd like to share."

"Oh, by all means, please, let's hear it." Sophia folded her arms across her chest in a closed-off manner. It was a bad sign for the start of their conversation, but Charlie chose to ignore it.

Instead, she dove into her theory about Curt and Monica. When they produced the ceramic vase, Detective Perez nearly combusted. Nelson had to assure her they'd taken every precaution not to touch the USB more than necessary and that they'd salvaged the evidence as best as possible.

It wasn't enough for her. She rounded on Charlie. "You're done. You hear me?"

Charlie blinked back at the woman, too shocked by her venomous tone to respond.

"No more investigating. No more pulling people into your crazy tangled web of conspiracy theories. And certainly no more tampering with evidence. You're lucky I don't charge you with interference in my case."

"I'm not—"

"No. You're not. Exactly." She took a step toward Charlie, her dark brown eyes narrowing to slits. "You're not doing anything but your job, Ms. Davis. And if you do more, Ben here will let me know."

Charlie sent a wide-eyed look toward the head of security, and he had the decency to look away, guilty. She couldn't be sure, but she didn't think this was the outcome he'd envisioned when he called the detective.

"Now, give me that vase. We're leaving and you're doing *nothing*. Right?" Charlie wouldn't give the woman the satisfaction of answering. She thought the detective might press the issue, but instead, she turned toward Nelson. "I'd expected better from you, Hall."

"Likewise," Nelson said.

Sophia flinched at that, but her mask was back in place within seconds. "We're out of there."

She strode toward the door but turned back to stare Charlie down. "You're done." Her last parting shot echoed through the office.

13

NELSON HELD out a fruity-looking drink to Charlie, and she accepted it. *La Cantina* was buzzing with life and activity despite it not even being five o'clock yet. It seemed the residents on the southern tip of the tied island didn't mind normal drinking times—or even days of the week.

"It's so busy here," she said, looking around.

"Doesn't matter what day it is—or what time—we like to have a good time down here." He grinned and slipped into the seat next to Charlie. They sat on the patio looking out toward the ocean. The breeze was just cool enough to make the shaded spot bearable in the increased heat of the day, and parts of her shoulders finally started to relax after being tensed from Detective Perez's searing statements earlier.

"I don't understand her," Charlie said, keeping her focus on the ocean.

"Who? Sophia?"

"You seem close. Want to fill me in? Did I step on a crack and invite her negative focus on me? Or what?"

He laughed and shook his head. "It's nothing like that. Or at least, I don't think so." He took a sip of his drink.

"Then what? I mean, I've been around police who don't like me. That kind of comes with the territory of being a P.I.—at least in some cases—but this is like the next level of dislike."

"Sophia is a hard woman to understand. She may feel threatened by you—"

"I work at a resort, for goodness sake! It's not like I'm gunning for her job."

"I know, but she may not see it that way."

"What other way could she see it? I'm just trying to be helpful."

"But it's her job, not yours."

Charlie turned to look at him finally. "And if your job was solving crimes, wouldn't you want all investigative minds on board? And what about Ben selling me out to her? What's that about?"

Nelson chuckled, sipping from his drink. Was it to give himself time to formulate an answer?

"What? What aren't you telling me? How do you know Detective Perez?" Charlie asked again.

"Sophia and I go back to the service."

"She was in the Army?"

"Yes. And, to be honest, she's always been like this."

"What? Territorial?"

"Shrewd and hardnosed." He sighed. "Charlie, think about it from her perspective—and before you get all huffy, I'm not standing up for her or picking sides. I think I just see it differently."

"Okay." Charlie dipped her head. She could be civil. "What do you see?"

"She's new to the department. She was in northern Florida and just moved to this new department to take an advanced position. This is her first big case and instead of running it her way—and showing her new co-workers that she's got things down—there's this P.I. who's interfering in her case."

"I'm not—"

"Not that you are, but that it could be seen that way."

"Well, why can't we have a civil conversation about everything?"

"Because Sophia doesn't do civil." There was a shadow that passed behind his eyes that worried Charlie. It showed her there was something Nelson was keeping back about this. What, though?

"So I should just back off?"

He looked over at her. "Would you?"

This time, Charlie took a drink to avoid answering the question right away. Could she step back? That wasn't in her nature. When she was on a case, she was a dog with a bone—or, better yet, a woman with a goal. She had a mission to uncover any and all subterfuge and get to the bottom of things. But then there was the roadblock of Sophia Perez.

Charlie was fairly certain the woman wouldn't hold back on charging her with obstruction if she found her working on the case again.

But would that stop her?

"No," she finally answered. "I'm not the kind of woman who can be relegated to the sidelines."

The hint of a smile tugged at the corner of Nelson's mouth. "I didn't think so."

"But I am worried. If she does charge me, I'm afraid that's the end of my career here at the Pearl Sands." She sighed. Was her involvement in a case really that important? "Maybe I should let it go."

"I think Sophia is about results," he finally said, breaking the easy silence that had fallen between them. "She's a woman of focus and force. If the outcome is achieved, she may not mind how as long as she gets the credit."

Charlie laughed. "And you know I don't care about the credit."

"Exactly."

Their eyes met over their drinks, and Nelson tilted his head. "What?" she asked, seeing a question behind the hazel.

"I'm just trying to figure you out, Charlie Davis."

She scrunched up her nose. "I'm just a woman who likes to solve mysteries, I guess." She shrugged. There was more to it than that, of course, but she didn't feel like wading into that territory with Nelson yet.

While she liked him and trusted him as far as investigations went, she wasn't sure she fully understood him. What motivated him? What was he really doing on Barnabe Island?

"I should get going," she said, standing and placing a twenty on the table.

"I've got it," he said, pushing the money toward her.

"No problem." She grinned. "Call it a good tip for Telma."

"I'm sure she's going to like that." Nelson stood. "Should I walk you back?"

"That's okay. I need to think. But, Nelson..." She stopped and turned to face him. "I'm sorry, again, about your shop and all your beautiful pottery."

He shrugged, rubbing a hand against his jaw. His stubble made a scratching sound as he did so. "It's okay. I have several pieces at my studio here I can take to *Ceramica*, but it'll be a while before I'm ready to even open again. I thought about adding a sign telling people to come down here, but I don't know how the residents here would feel about that."

"True. It is like a hidden gem here."

"It is. I'm glad you found it." His eyes warmed to her, and she forced herself to break away.

"Bye, Nelson."

He waved her off, and she started back toward the resort on foot. The sand of the beach squished between her toes. Nelson was an enigma, and Detective Perez was a puzzle. How had she landed herself in the middle of all of this?

But the better question was, could she put an end to the investigation before Detective Perez put an end to her?

THE WALK back had sufficed to clear her head. Charlie knew better than to let a bully get to her. While Detective Perez likely meant well in most respects, cautioning her not to continue in her investigation only did one thing: inspire Charlie to work harder to get to the bottom of it all.

Now there was the added pressure of secrecy, though. She had a feeling Ben Simmons was more interested in looking good to the boss, and perhaps getting Charlie thrown back to her initial place as concierge, than making a new friend. While she respected his drive to do his job well, she knew he had made a crucial mistake. He'd betrayed her trust.

Charlie checked her phone and sent off another text. The next step of her plan was falling into place, but she had to make it look almost accidental. It would be hard, but not impossible, and she could only hope that the security office wouldn't be looking too closely at the Seaview Café.

Charlie slipped inside and ordered an iced coffee. She took a seat at the very back corner. She'd specifically looked at the cameras in a few key locations when she'd first been introduced to the security office and had taken note of two things.

What areas were under surveillance—which was almost everywhere in the resort—as well as where the cameras might be less than effective. She hadn't had a chance to categorize much more than the café and the path to her own residence in the short time she'd been in the office with Ben the first time, but her memory was sharp and she knew that the seat she'd chosen was the least visible.

It felt a little like paranoia, sitting in the back corner of the café waiting for a clandestine meeting, but Charlie had no other alternatives. At least, none that she could see easily, and she decided that if this was the last case she worked at the Pearl Sands, then that would be that.

A twinge of guilt shot through her. She knew her job was concierge—that was what she'd been hired to—and while she was making it, she wouldn't say she was thriving at the job. She'd gotten her workload done, though most of the time that was after hours when she finally had time away from guests to focus on the work. Was she letting the resort down by trying to catch a killer? Then again, Felipe had wanted her help.

"Charlie?" Monica's soft voice broke into her concentration, and she looked up to see the young woman.

"Have a seat. Thanks for meeting with me."

"Your message said it was urgent—and for me not to bring Will. What is this about?"

Charlie had hoped the woman wouldn't get too suspicious, but it was imperative she met with her without her husband present. "I need to ask you some hard questions."

"What are you talking about?"

"I know you stole the USB and hid it in the bottom of your pottery vase."

Monica's eyes went wide. "I— I— How did you know?"

"I found it. And I assume the police will be reaching out to you soon, but I needed to speak with you first because I want to know the truth."

"What are you talking about?"

Charlie caught the quick look away that signaled Monica was lying. She knew exactly what Charlie was talking about. "Come on, Monica. I know that the night the USB was stolen, you went back to your room to grab a wrap but left the door unlocked. Were you stealing it to give to Curt?"

Monica's expression went blank. "Curt—like Curt Mulroney? What are you talking about?"

Charlie's eyes narrowed. Perhaps she'd made the wrong assumption. Monica's surprise seemed genuine. "Curt wasn't helping you steal the USB?"

Monica's lower lip trembled and she pressed a fist to it, but her shoulders began to shake and tears fell. "I had no choice."

"What happened, Monica?"

"It started with an email."

Charlie leaned forward. Finally, she was getting the truth. "From who?"

"It was from Drake—but from an email address I didn't recognize. He said that he had information on Will he was going to give to the media. That it would ruin Will's career and me along with it, but he wouldn't release it if I stole Will's NFTs." She swiped tears away. "I love Will, but I knew something was going on. He's been acting so strangely, and it was enough to make me believe what Drake said."

"He didn't give you evidence or tell you what his information was?"

"No." Monica shook her head. "And honestly, I didn't want to know."

Charlie nodded. Sometimes ignorance *was* bliss. "What happened next?"

"We kind of planned it all through email. He told me it should happen at the resort so that it would be public and visible, and I agreed. What you saw—me going back for my shawl—was me getting the USB and messing up a few things. I did leave the door open and figured someone might think it was on accident, you know?"

"But what did you do with the USB then?"

"I had it with me." She flushed and shook her head. "It was stupid, but I didn't know where I could hide it in the room, you know?"

Charlie nodded. "What happened next?"

"I hid it in our room, at the bottom of my luggage."

"Did you know Drake was coming to the resort? Had he arranged to get the USB?"

"No." Monica shook her head violently and stared Charlie down. "I had no clue he'd be here. It was shocking, and I wanted to confront him. I'd done what he asked and was going to mail it like he'd said, but there was never a chance. And he was with his new girlfriend."

"He didn't try to talk to you?"

"No. I figured he didn't want anyone thinking we were still communicating."

"So, the night he died…" Charlie left it open for Monica to fill in the holes.

"I was going to confront him. I brought the USB with me, but then Will was being so sweet and wanted to go back to our room. I was terrified he'd find it on me, so…I stuck it in some clay, at the bottom. I thought I could go back for it."

"And you didn't see anyone around the pottery area?" Charlie still couldn't figure out the timeline.

"That was the really strange part." Monica played with the strap of her small clutch. "Will and I were back at the pottery area, like we said, but he left early for that call and that was my chance. I put the USB in the bottom of the pot and left. No one was around."

Charlie nodded, wondering how this all connected. "Then you left to take a walk on the beach."

"Yes. I saw Drake and he was alone—we both were—and I confronted him. He was so drunk, I honestly wasn't sure if I would get anything from him, but I told him I had the USB and it was safe in the clay. I'd get it to him when I could and that if I'd known we could meet on the beach, I would have brought it, and we'd be done with this whole thing."

"What did he say to that?" Charlie was beginning to see something in Monica's story that worried her. Her next words would confirm or alleviate her suspicions.

"It was the weirdest thing. Maybe he was more drunk than I knew, but he acted like he had no idea what I was talking about. I got so mad—it was just like him to pull something like this—so I left."

"He didn't try to follow you?"

"Nope. I went to look for Will. I couldn't find him and started to worry that I'd jeopardized him—well, more than I already had by taking the USB—so I went back to the beach to talk to Drake. I was going to apologize and make sure we were okay, that he wouldn't release the information, but..."

Charlie knew what had happened after that. "He was dead."

"Exactly. I mean, I didn't want him dead, but it was a bit of a relief. You know?" Monica met Charlie's gaze with a vulnerable look. "I assumed all our troubles would be fixed, but now the police suspect me and, Charlie, I *stole* the USB. They're going to find those emails and think that I killed Drake. That detective even said that I could have done it with how drunk he was, but I didn't kill him. I may not have liked him, but I'm not a killer."

Charlie nodded. She saw what she thought was truth in the young woman's eyes, but if she didn't kill Drake, someone else did. They had trashed the pottery class area and broken into Nelson's shop. And they were still on the loose.

14

CHARLIE'S GUT instincts were warring with one another. Monica had left their conversation in a hurricane of tears, but she had convinced Charlie of her innocence for the murder.

She'd thought to call Detective Perez about Monica's confession about the theft, but at this point, she was certain the detective would get evidence off of the vase that would link back to Monica. If not, Charlie would speak up, but having the young woman out of jail for the time being was helpful. It meant the killer wouldn't start to feel them narrowing in on them—yet.

The problem was, Charlie was fairly certain that Drake hadn't been the person blackmailing Monica. Not only had he *not* admitted it when Monica confronted him, he also hadn't asked for the USB, which Charlie assumed would have been his top priority once she'd procured it.

If it wasn't Drake, then who was posing as Drake?

Standing up from the table, Charlie tossed her paper coffee cup in the trash and left the Seaview Café. She wasn't sure where she was heading next. Work beckoned, and she knew there were still a few items that needed clearing up for a few weekend guests, but there was something ticking at the back of her mind. Some detail she hadn't resolved yet, though it eluded her at the moment.

She wasn't watching where she was going and nearly ran into a man before she caught herself. When she looked up, she saw that it was Lucas Vello.

"Mr. Vello, good afternoon."

His eyes narrowed. "Afternoon."

"Charlie Davis—from the concierge desk."

"Ah, yes. Right. Hello again."

"Hello." Her pulse ticked up as a thought occurred. "You run ArtistOcean, right?"

He looked pleased to be recognized. "I do. Are you an artist or collector?"

"Neither," she admitted with a laugh. "I do have a question for you regarding Will Chrisman."

His eyebrows rose. "Oh?"

"I work here at the resort, but I used to be a private investigator. Perhaps old habits die hard, but I'm wondering why you're still here."

"Are you trying to kick me out of the Pearl Sands?" His chuckle was indulgent.

"Not at all." She warmed her words with a smile. "But I am wondering why you, a busy man, would stay when Will's art is no longer available. I mean, his NFTs were stolen, weren't they?"

"You seem to know a lot about this. And about me." His suspicion mingled with curiosity.

"I do, but I've been looking into the disappearance of his USB for the resort—a little freelance work my boss, the Pearl Sands manager, asked me to do."

"I see. And have you found it?"

"It's slipped through my grasp," she answered honestly, thinking of the vase in Detective Perez's hands. "So, if they are gone and there is no hope of recovery, I assume your deal would be off? That's me guessing you had a deal," she added with a wink.

Lucas looked around the bright walkway as if checking for listening ears before he turned back to Charlie. "The thing with art is that it is never done until the artist is. Will may not have his original NFTs at the moment—my team is working on recovery as we speak—but he is not dead." His smile widened. "If there is a chance he'll create more, I'll work with him."

"That's logical," she said. She held his gaze. "What about the claims that he's using AI-created art in his pieces? More than is acceptable for an artist-designed piece?"

Lucas didn't blink. "Baseless claims unless there is proof to back it up."

"But you knew about the accusations."

"Curt came to see me—"

"Curt Mulroney?"

He nodded. "He said that there were rumors around about Will's digital art and that I needed to be careful."

"Was he threatening you?"

"Honestly? I'm not sure. Curt seemed…" He searched for the word. "Desperate."

"To keep Will at his gallery?" At Lucas's nod, she pressed. "But why would Will have to choose? You don't deal in physical art, so what's the issue?"

"It was Will. He wanted his physical paintings—the ones that hadn't yet sold—back. He wanted to move away from Curt and join ArtistOcean. We are one of the world's leading digital art galleries, you know." His smug expression deepened.

"I've heard." Charlie tried to make sense of it all.

"The thing is, by signing with me, I would agree to buy out the rest of his contract with Curt. There wasn't much left, but it was enough that it would solidify our deal, and Will would be free to digitally create. We're a much freer gallery space anyway."

"I see." And Charlie was starting to see. Will was locked into a contract with Curt, yet he was willing to sign a new deal, despite the rumors about his art, if that meant Lucas would buy Curt out. A number, Charlie guessed, that was lower than what Curt could get for the rest of Will's paintings.

"I really do need to go. Online meeting in fifteen."

"Thank you so much for your time, Mr. Vello."

He dipped his head and slipped away, but she stayed rooted to the spot. Curt wanted—perhaps needed—Will's business. But why? There was more going on beneath the surface, she was sure of it, but only Curt could clear things up.

She pulled out her phone and sent off a text. It was time to finally talk to Curt.

CURT MULRONEY STEPPED into Pinnacle and looked around with a practiced eye. She could tell he suspected nothing and that comforted her. She needed him to be off his guard somewhat. He toured through the right side of the gallery, pausing in a few places, and she waited in her partially hidden spot at the back of the gallery.

When Curt drew closer, she took her opportunity. "Hello, Mr. Mulroney."

"You." He looked surprised to see her, if not a little frustrated. "Was this all a ruse?"

"I'm afraid I did take a bit of creative license to get you here, but I just want to talk."

"Do I need a lawyer?" The way he said it clued her into the fact that he was being sarcastic, but she took the bait.

"I don't know. Did you do anything that could get you arrested?"

"To be clear, you're a private investigator, are you not?"

"I am." She took a step. "Did Monica tell you that?"

"Monica?" He looked genuinely surprised. "No, it's just the way you've been lurking in dark corners and accosting everyone. It reeks of investigation that's not sanctioned by the police."

"Mr. Mulroney, if you could answer a few questions, that would help me to reframe my thinking on this whole case."

"What do you mean?"

Charlie gauged how much she wanted to tell him. "What is it you hoped to accomplish with Will by coming to the Pearl Sands? I mean, he's on his honeymoon and yet you thought you could convince him to, what, keep his art with you? From what I understand, he's already made up his mind about that."

"He hasn't." His repose was quick and, she assumed, made without thought. "Or at least, I don't think he has." Curt shifted from one foot to the other and finally crossed his arms. "Despite the fact I don't *want* to cooperate with you,

I will tell you this. Will's art is a gift, and my hope was to convince him to keep it in my gallery for the sake of humanity."

"Such a lofty aspiration." She narrowed her eyes. "But that's not the only reason."

"No, he's well-known, and it would be foolish of me to let him go without a fight."

He still wasn't telling the truth. She could tell by the way he averted his gaze when he answered. "Did that fight extend to murder?"

Curt looked like she'd slapped him. "Absolutely not. Who do you think I am?"

"A desperate man, though I still don't know why."

"I'm not *that* desperate." He looked away again. "But I will tell you this for the sake of your understanding and that only. You must promise me word of this will not spread."

"As long as it's not illegal, then I give you my word."

"It's nothing like that." He looked around the room, an image of longing portrayed on his face. "I'm close to losing the Rockford. I don't like to admit it in public, but if you insist on knowing my reasons then know I am desperate in a sense—I need his art in order for my gallery to stay afloat—but I am not desperate in the way you mean. My gallery means everything to me, and I will do what I can to ensure it survives this, but there would be no reason for me to kill Mr. Brown. I hardly knew him and see no benefit to any of it."

She searched his features. Was he telling the truth? Did he really not know about the digital art?

"Having Will's paintings in the Rockford would really guarantee its success?"

"Nothing in the art world is a guarantee, but it would help. People often come in even just to see them and then end up purchasing something of lower quality. It keeps us afloat. And if I were to sell one, well, that would be beneficial as well. Why would I risk a good life by killing some random man?"

"I don't think you would." She gave him the answer to his question, but she also wasn't fully convinced. It was still possible that he'd known about Drake and his insinuation about Will's art.

If Charlie had to guess, using AI art and claiming it as your own could call into question *all* of Will's art. That wouldn't be a good look for the Rockford Gallery. If Curt was as fierce about protecting it as he said, if he'd learned about Drake's threats, could he have offered to take care of the problem if Will would stay on with the gallery?

"Now, if that is all, I'll be leaving. I do have a gallery to run —for the time it stays afloat." He moved to step past her but paused. "If there is any goodness in you and you talk with Will… Please let him know that I would be more than generous with him if he'd keep his art in the Rockford."

She blinked. "I don't think it would mean anything coming from me. I'm sorry, Mr. Mulroney."

He huffed a half-chuckle, half-breath. "I had to try."

He left in a cloud of too-strong, cheap cologne, and Charlie turned to watch him go. She sensed Michael behind her a few moments later.

"What did you make of that?" She turned to face Michael, who she'd asked to listen in to see if he caught the other gallery owner in any type of lie.

"He sounded genuine and, while I'm loath to share gossip, I have heard rumors about Rockford and its insolvency." Michael offered a shrug. "It also makes sense that Will's paintings would bring in other customers and could be the reason he's going so hard after keeping Will at the Rockford."

"Is it not possible for Will to do both? Keep his physical art somewhere and his digital elsewhere? I've talked to Lucas Vello, and he seems to think Will didn't want that."

"It's up to personal taste, I suppose. Most artists want their art in as many places as possible. It's my understanding Will hasn't painted anything at all for several years and that his original digital art was not well received."

"Which could be why he turned to AI art," Charlie mused.

"There's another rumor," Michael said. He bit his lip, and Charlie could tell he wasn't sure if he should share or not.

"Are we talking gossip or something that *could* be seen as accurate?"

"Depends on who you ask."

"What do *you* think of it?" She held his gaze.

"While it is out there as a theory, it does make me wonder."

She gauged his response. "If you feel comfortable, why don't you tell me and I'll gauge whether or not I think it's pertinent?"

He took a breath. "There is a rumor going around on some art forums—might even be more of a guess or conspiracy theory—suggesting that Will didn't even paint his original paintings. People have done what they call a "deep dive" into his past and found that his mother was an art major in college, but she dropped out to raise him as a single mother."

Charlie had a feeling she could see where this was going but wouldn't write it off just because it was a theory. Sometimes, the most outlandish theories were based in truth. "They think the art was hers?"

"Yes. They think that he knew just enough to make it look as if he painted them and then he started selling them at farmers' markets. He got attention when well-known artist in the Boston area saw his work, and the rest is history. He was on major networks talking about his art—his process—and basking in the glow of selling art for thousands of dollars."

"But surely something like that could be verified?"

"There isn't a great way to check the veracity of it—short of making Will sit down and paint in front of you—because he is a self-proclaimed reclusive artist. He only paints at home and won't allow anyone to watch him until the painting is done."

"His mother never said anything?"

"This is where things get interesting." Michael looked to be warming to the topic. "She was diagnosed with early onset dementia. He stayed home to take care of her, telling the world his art was funding her care, but then she died about four years ago."

"No more art—assuming the theory is true."

"Just about the time his mother passed away. The timeline fits, but again, there is no way to prove it."

"Why wouldn't he want to sell the paintings he has, then? It doesn't make sense that he would pull them from the Rockford."

"I'd wondered that too," Michael admitted. "There's obviously no answer—unless Will admits to one—but my guess would be he either doesn't want them to be available for public viewing if he's afraid the truth will come out or—and this could be 'and' as well—he wants to drive up their price."

"Since he's well-known in name."

"That, and holding on to them for a few years, he'd be able to fetch a higher price and percentage from someone else selling them for him when it is clear he is no longer doing physical paintings."

Charlie tilted her head. "He wouldn't be afraid of his digital art taking over for the physical?"

"They are such different mediums and styles that I don't think it could come to that."

Charlie brought the conversation back to Curt. "Do you think it's possible Curt knew about Drake Brown's blackmail? Your best guess, that is," she clarified.

"I'm not sure. From what he said, I would guess no, just because he's still going at Will pretty hard to keep his contract. It's strange to me, though." Michael took a deep breath. "The Rockford is known for being exclusive, and I think that's what's causing the damage."

"How so?" Charlie knew nothing about art galleries, but she was interested to learn.

"If he were to open slots up, like the ones taken by Will's paintings, to local artists, I think he would sell a lot more. His price tags are so exorbitant that it's no wonder he's not having success."

"That does seem like a shortcoming. Would that have any bearing on his singular focus on Will? He's so high-end that Drake's threat would be detrimental to him?"

"Honestly? I would assume Curt would want to distance himself from an artist that could be involved in a scandal. Even the mere mention of it would be enough...even without proof."

"Then again, with Drake out of the way, there would be no scandal," she said, more to herself than Michael. "Thank you. Not only for the use of the gallery but for your expertise."

"Anything I can do to help. I think I get why my sister and Stephen like this stuff."

"Stuff?"

"True crime." He grinned.

"It has its ups and downs." Charlie considered what she'd learned, and a truth began to reveal itself. It was quickly followed by reality. "I need to go."

"All right. Let me know how things turn out?"

She grinned. "Oh, I will. I think the end is closer than we think."

15

CHARLIE WATCHED Will and Monica wheel their bags into the resort lobby. A twinge of regret shot through her at their easygoing repartee, but she knew she'd done what she had to. It was time for her to take the next step.

"Good morning, Mr. and Mrs. Chrisman," she said in her most cheerful voice. "Checking out?"

Monica looked tired, but she still clutched Will's hand like a lifeline. "Yes, I suppose all honeymoons have to come to an end."

"They do." Charlie met Will's gaze. "Did all of your business get wrapped up?"

His smile was wide. "It did. I'm ending my contract with Rockford and moving on with ArtistOcean. Good things lay ahead."

"That is fortuitous. All this happened in one honeymoon?" Charlie laughed, and Will joined her. Monica remained more subdued. Was she thinking about what she'd admitted to Charlie about the USB drive?

"I did have one last thing I needed to clear up with you both, if you'll follow me to a more private office?"

A shadow passed behind Monica's eyes, but Will seemed more intrigued than concerned. "Sure," he said.

"This way." Charlie led them down a hall to the same conference room Detective Don Neal had used when interrogating witnesses from the case months ago. It felt wrong slipping into a chair across from Will and Monica, their backs to the door, but she pushed those feelings aside.

Charlie pulled out a black folder from her bag and set it on the table. Her gaze shifted to the small window just above Monica's shoulder, and her nod was slow but deliberate.

"What's this about?" Will asked. He still appeared unconcerned.

"It's about fakes, Mr. Chrisman." Detective Perez stepped into the room as Charlie opened the folder and pulled out printed copies of Will's NFT art.

"I— What are you doing here? I want a lawyer." Will spat the words the instant the detective sat down next to Charlie.

"Wait, Will. Just hold on." Monica looked from her new husband to the photos Charlie had laid out on the table. "Look."

He leaned forward, his brow winkling in worry now. "What— Where is this from?"

"As you can see, the areas of concern are marked in red," Detective Perez began. "Not only is this AI-generated art you're passing off as your own without revealing its origin, there is evidence to tie you to overseas payments to an artist in Ukraine that created these images for you."

"That's—" He shut his mouth.

"We know, *lawyer*, but first, you can hear us out," she said.

Charlie almost did a double-take when the woman said "us" and then turned to face Charlie as if to say, "Go on, you're next."

"It took a while for me to piece it together because you were clever—though I hate to give you that compliment." Charlie glanced at the detective, but she was staring down the couple. "I think it started out as simply blackmail—not that that is ever simple. Drake came to you and claimed he'd found a way to prove you'd used AI art. Still not sure *how* he found that out, but I'm sure Detective Perez will get there." Charlie tamped down her smile. "You might have given in at first, but it's clear that Drake wanted more and more from you. He even came to the Pearl Sands—probably on your dime—to rub it in your face."

"But Drake emailed *me*!" Monica burst out.

Will's hand landed on her shoulder in a vice-like grip. "Stop talking," he said through clenched teeth.

"I thought so too, and yes, the detective does know everything you told me Monica." Monica flushed, and Will's gaze shot daggers at her. "But it didn't add up. He told you to steal it, but in reality, that was Will posing as Drake. It makes sense when you revisit what you told me about how he responded to you on the beach. He had no idea you had taken the USB."

"But—"

"Mon, stop it," Will growled.

"No. It's not right. I— I was emailing with Drake," she pleaded with them.

"The next question I had was who would wreck the pottery to look for the USB? Couldn't have been Drake, he was killed around that time. And then the pieces fell into place. Will had seen you leave while he was on a call and, when he saw you talking to your ex-boyfriend, I'm sure he started to panic." Charlie met Will's fiery gaze. "He overheard where you'd hidden the USB, and he had to make sure it never saw the light of day. He searched but couldn't find it because he hadn't been there when you put the pot in the locker. Later, I believe he hired someone to break into *Ceramica* to find it, but they didn't know to look in the kiln, which is how we got these copies."

"The trail of payments is clear, Mr. Chrisman," Detective Perez jumped in. "We're also having your physical paintings analyzed by a specialist to see if we can connect it with those of your mother's older paintings."

"They're mine!" he all but screamed.

"They may be, but there are a lot of factors in this, like if your mother knew you were selling her art or if that was yet another con. Now, you asked for a lawyer and we'll get you one—at the station." The detective stood up. "You're coming with us as well, Mrs. Chrisman."

The look of hurt and betrayal that Monica cast toward her husband broke Charlie, but there was nothing else to say.

The truth was out, and while Lucas Vello and Curt Mulroney would be out an artist, at least they wouldn't be in jail.

16

THE SOUNDS of soft jazz played over the hidden speakers at the Rockford Gallery, and Charlie watched Curt Mulroney circle through the different areas talking and laughing with his new patrons. It had only been two weeks since Will and Monica were taken from the Pearl Sands in handcuffs, but Charlie was impressed to see the new leaf the gallery owner had turned over.

"Ah, there is the lady of the hour," he said, holding up a glass of champagne to her. He wore a crisp new suit and had a refreshed look to him. "This would have been a closing party without your suggestions."

"Not mine," she reminded him. "Michael Gutierrez."

"Yes, well, him and your friend Nelson have truly saved the day."

Charlie's gaze traveled the room to find Nelson at one end, speaking with a group of three women. They all laughed at something he said, and Charlie felt her stomach tighten.

"I assume things are going well?" she asked.

"Marvelous," Curt said, sipping from his glass. "The local artists have already brought in a good bit of income in only a week of being featured here and while their prices are lower—something I still dislike—I find that they are more apt to sell and tourists are willing to buy them. I'd call that a win-win."

"Me too. I'm glad to hear it."

He nodded and walked to the next group with a flourish of exaggerated welcome.

Charlie looked back at the piece in front of her. It was a lovely seaside scene that reminded her of Barnabe Island. The soft tones and modern edge to it made the scene look like any beach you might want to remember in Florida, but the tag told the truth.

"You like this one?" Nelson's low voice registered near her ear, and she turned to face him with a grin.

"I do. Thank you." She accepted the fluted glass he offered.

"I told you we'd get that drink eventually."

Her laugh filled the space between them. "I don't think this counts."

"Oh, so you want to keep it on the calendar, then? Some time, some day?"

She let her eyes roam over his face before answering. "Sure."

"Good." His resounding smile shifted as he took in the piece. "This is by my friend, Briana Branson. Remember, I told you about her?"

"I do remember. I assume you're responsible for her being here? In the Rockford?"

"Maybe." He grinned. "But she's talented enough. She just needed a stage and, while I thought she may need time to adjust, she's done well."

Charlie admired the way Nelson looked out for his friends and agreed that the young woman was indeed talented.

They admired the piece for a few minutes more. The front door opened again, and Felipe walked in. Nelson sighed beside her.

"Someday, you're going to tell me what it is between you and Felipe. *And* you're going to tell me the rest of the story with Sophia Perez."

Nelson's eyebrows narrowed. "That's demanding for someone who keeps me in the dark about her past."

She felt the sting of his admonishing words and wondered if he was right. Was she asking too much of him? Assuming he should be truthful with her when, in reality, their friendship only offered a portion of that. The same portion she'd afforded him?

If asking him to open up to her meant he would only do so if she responded in kind, it felt like too big of a step in that moment.

"Perhaps you're right. Excuse me." Turning her back on Nelson, Charlie greeted Felipe, who was already walking her way.

"I see Mr. Hall is here admiring his work."

Charlie frowned. "Oh?"

"He has worked with Briana for years now. This is a huge achievement for them both."

Charlie blinked. "Worked with... Does he paint?" Charlie reeled a little. Nelson hadn't mentioned that aspect of his assistance with Briana.

"He does many things." Felipe took a flute of champagne as a waiter walked past. "But... A toast to you, Ms. Davis. To yet another case solved."

She blushed and took a sip. "Thank you, but it was a group effort."

"I heard. Valentina was involved, Michael her brother, and there was even trouble with Ben."

Charlie hadn't seen Felipe around the resort nearly at all during the case, and now he showed up knowing more than she'd expected. "How did you know?"

"I was absent for personal reasons," he said, looking down and away, "but I kept in touch. I am sorry he undercut you as he did. I have spoken with him about this."

"You didn't have to."

"But I did. He must understand that you are part of a team that goes beyond what you do. His job is not in danger, and I would prefer for him to work *with* you than against you."

"I would like that as well." Charlie took in the new painting in front of them, but she didn't really see it. "Are you all right, Felipe?"

He'd mentioned personal reasons, but she'd seen it before he said anything. He wasn't his usual charming self.

"It is my aunt—my mother's youngest sister from a second marriage her father had. She is ill, and I have been struggling to come to terms that I am not the best to give her the care she needs. I spent last week transitioning her to a top-rated care facility, but it was difficult. She is easily confused, and I needed to be there until she was settled in."

His absence suddenly made sense, but it also tugged at her heartstrings. "I'm so sorry to hear that."

"She is doing better, thankfully, and will be back to normal soon, I'm sure."

"Is there anything you need?" She placed a hand on his arm.

"No, but thank you."

"Well, let me know if I can do anything."

"I will. And, Charlie?"

She paused before she went to join Valentina and Stephen on the other side of the room.

"I will stop intruding on your work if you would rather not help in cases that come up. Just one word and I will never ask again."

She found his offer to be so kind, and so unexpected in showing her the full picture of what he saw, that she said, "You know, I'm good with helping out in my capacity for now, but I do have a favor. Perhaps we can discuss it over drinks this weekend?"

His smile was almost giddy and lit up the room. It showed her another side of Felipe where he wasn't being the anxious, harried boss. It also helped her relax about the offer she'd just made. It was time to broach the subject of Juliana joining her team—if the young woman agreed.

"I would love that. You can let me know your availability and preferred location, and I'll meet you there."

She appreciated that he didn't assume it was a date— which it wasn't, not really—and nodded her agreement. "I will."

THE NEXT MORNING, Charlie heard a knock on the door. The clock read just a few minutes past seven in the morning, and she was thankful she had already been up and dressed. She was usually up early.

Upon opening the door, Charlie felt her jaw drop. "Detective Perez?"

The woman offered a half-smirk and a cup of coffee. "Want to sit on the beach?"

There were too many questions jumbling around in her head to pick just one, so Charlie closed the door behind her and accepted the coffee without a word. They walked down the path that grew increasingly sandy and soon reached the first recliners toward the back of the beach area.

Taking a seat facing the water, Charlie took a sip of the bitter brew. "Good coffee."

"Believe it or not, my husband made it."

Charlie sent a sideways glance at the woman. Was she opening up to her? "He did a good job."

"So he tells me." She sipped her own coffee and stared into the distance. "I think we got off on the wrong foot."

Charlie laughed. "You could say that."

"I also think I misjudged you."

"Oh?" Charlie tuned to face the woman, who did likewise.

"I've dealt with private investigators in the past, and it hasn't been a positive experience. They've sought out their own glory and tried to get their stamp on the case so that it could bring in more cases for them."

"I don't care about recognition. I only care about the truth."

"Spoken like a cop."

Charlie had a feeling the detective had done her research on Charlie's past. "In a former time, yes, but the mentality stuck."

"I can tell. That, and Nelson vouched for you." The way Detective Perez said it was a challenge.

"And exactly how do you know Nelson?" Charlie said, accepting the challenge.

"He was married to my sister, Gabriella." She looked back out at the ocean.

Was. That word stuck with Charlie.

"He's a good guy," the detective finally said. "And now I know that you're a good P.I. as well. You didn't have to call me when you confronted Will and Monica. You could have busted the case wide open to the media and claimed your spot of fame, but you didn't. You compiled your information in a neat and orderly manner and brought me in on it. That's why I let you be in the room with me. I knew I could trust you."

"You can." Charlie didn't feel the need to say anything else.

"Well..." Detective Perez stood. "Don't take advantage of it."

Charlie laughed, the feeling easy and free in that moment because she was starting to see just who Sophia Perez was, and she liked her.

"Keep in touch if things go down here," she said.

"I will. And thanks for the coffee, Sophia."

"Maybe we'll do it again, Charlie." Sophia grinned. "You've got the better view."

Thanks for reading *Clues in the Clay*. We hope you enjoyed this adventure with Charlie, the Pearl Sands Resort, and, of course, Cal the mischievous monkey. If you could take a minute and leave a review for me on Amazon and/or Goodreads, that would be really nice :)

Be sure to check out the next book, ***Theft in the Theater***, and all the books in the Pearl Sands series on Amazon.

Also, be sure to check out the Florida Keys Bed and Breakfast Cozy Mystery series where we first met Charlene. The first book in that series is called *Murder Mystery Book Club* and it has over 2400 five star reviews on Amazon (and over 4800 total reviews).

If you would like to know about future cozy mysteries by me and the other authors at Fairfield Publishing, make sure to sign up for our Cozy Mystery Newsletter. We will send you our FREE Cozy Mystery Starter Library just for signing up. All the details are on the next page.

FAIRFIELD COZY MYSTERY NEWSLETTER

Make sure you sign up for the Fairfield Cozy Mystery Newsletter so you can keep up with our latest releases. When you sign up, **we will send you our FREE Cozy Mystery Starter Library!**

FairfieldPublishing.com/cozy-newsletter/

Made in the USA
Middletown, DE
19 February 2025